The Kindest use a Knife

Also by Vanessa Jones

TWELVE

VANESSA JONES

The Kindest use a Knife

Flamingo

An Imprint of HarperCollins*Publishers*

Flamingo
An imprint of HarperCollins*Publishers*
77–85 Fulham Palace Road,
Hammersmith, London W6 8JB

Flamingo is a registered trade mark of
HarperCollins Publishers Limited

www.**fire**and**water**.com

Published by Flamingo 2003
9 8 7 6 5 4 3 2 1

First published in Great Britain by
Flamingo 2002

This novel is entirely a work of fiction.
The names, characters and incidents portrayed in it are
the work of the author's imagination. Any resemblance to
actual persons, living or dead, events or localities is
entirely coincidental.

Photograph of Vanessa Jones © Paul Cooper

ISBN 0 00 655239 0

Set in Minion and Din Mittelschrift by
Palimpsest Book Production Limited, Polmont, Stirlingshire

Printed and bound in Great Britain by
Clays Ltd, St Ives plc

for Ben and Jane

The Kindest use a Knife

Yet each man kills the thing he loves,
By each let this be heard,
Some do it with a bitter look,
Some with a flattering word.
The coward does it with a kiss,
The brave man with a sword!

Some kill their love when they are young,
And some when they are old;
Some strangle with the hands of Lust,
Some with the hands of Gold:
The kindest use a knife, because
The dead so soon grow cold.

from 'The Ballad of Reading Gaol' OSCAR WILDE

PART ONE

One

I was in the club that night with a boy I had met a few weeks before at a lunchtime recital. He was playing the clarinet. Not that night (although he did take me home with him later and give me a bit of Mozart, after some gentle persuasion), no, that night I took him for dinner in an undistinguished restaurant and we went to the club afterwards for a drink. James was at the bar, surprised to see me. He said, 'Peter! I thought you hated this place.'

I said, 'I do. But Joseph and I were just having dinner and he said he'd never been here before.' Joseph blushed. 'And I *am* still a member.'

'God knows why.'

'They do a nice lunch.'

This length of conversation is about all I can stand with James so I was glad to see Lee arrive, seconds later. I was facing the door and saw him first, but something on my face must have mirrored, in shock, the extreme expression on Lee's – for James saw it and turned around. He would have said 'Hi' in his normal way (for a nanosecond his mouth made that twitch) but he noticed in Lee the reason for my instant of shock: he was huge, shuddering, his face so reddened with anger it was almost black, he came over to James and pushed a finger and thumb under his jaw, he said, 'You've gone too far this time,' shouted, 'You've gone too far,' and, jabbing a finger in James's face, 'You're over.' Then he was gone. It all happened so quickly, there was barely anything to recover from. He was gone. Two days later he was dead. It all happened so quickly.

Two

This time, though, there is a lot to recover from. I surprise myself with the extent of my mourning. A year on and I still catch myself crying (albeit not so often) in the middle of some mundane task and I wonder, does this mean I loved him? When he was alive it was the same: do I love him? I met him at least twice a week for over five years, that's a habit to break; and then there's the shock of it too, I suppose. Death like that, it's something I read about, something I see on TV, something that happens, but not to me. It's not a part of my life.

Three

James is saying, 'I wasn't leaving, I was arriving.' He looks pale and nervous inside his Prada suit. There is something about his skin that I've always disliked, it is creamy white, almost translucent, the kind that never goes brown in the sun, only sweats. His blue eyes dart around the courtroom. He can't look directly at the man asking these questions. But then, he can't look directly at anybody.

'I put it to you,' says the prosecuting lawyer, 'that you were leaving—'

'No,' says James.

'—Having taken cocaine with your friend, having laced

his beer with sleeping pills, having waited until he passed out and then,' and here he pauses for maximum effect, 'having injected your friend with an empty syringe.' James shakes his head. Gazes round the room. He can't believe this is happening to him. Who can help him? 'You waited until you were sure he was dead,' says his interrogator, 'and then you left, and somebody saw you leave, at half past nine.'

'I wasn't leaving, I was arriving,' says James, almost in a whisper.

Four

This story, the bigger story, fragments of moments I spent with Lee have been retelling themselves, unfolding themselves, flashing into my head until I can't remember any longer how much is false how much is fact, how much of Lee is left. Memories are erratic, but is there a method behind their selection? Do I tell myself, somewhere, to discard all those with element x? Then how much of Lee is left? James's eyes are peering out from his expensive suit, pale and watering behind his glasses, his neck is scrawny like a chicken's, his head jutting forward anxiously like a chicken's, his hair even thinner under the stress. No matter the outcome, what an horrific experience. I imagine Lee delighted. His was always such a keen sense of justice.

Five

Things I almost noticed but thought I shouldn't – the blue in the grey of his eyes, the exact dark brown of his hair

– come to me unexpectedly and are gone just as quickly, things I didn't think I'd ever need to notice. His fingers rest on his knees, such long fingers, the last two on his left hand jutting slightly after the accident; tall legs in dark-blue jeans; V-neck sweaters worn with nothing underneath; his waist which was extended like a dancer's. I see his body cambered round his cello, although I never actually saw it like that. He didn't play the cello again after his accident, and that was before we met. He didn't make love again either. Perhaps he might have done with Gina. Perhaps he might have done had James not messed it up. But what does that matter now? His body is ash.

Six

Except that it does matter to this court, to these jurors, to me who can think of little else. Blame must be apportioned, and not just for his death; for his life. He was easily led, I always thought, but that wasn't true, I couldn't lead him. He let James do that, let everything go, let me down, let Gina . . . I am hot with anger until I remember that he's paid for it. He came storming round to see me the day after his party for her, no sleep, still drunk, still coked off his head. He said 'I can't handle this' after only ten minutes and stormed out again. Long legs in dark jeans. There she is sitting on the left. It might be a church, this courtroom, this might be a wedding, Bride or Groom? James is left, Lee is right; Gina's sitting on the left. He's paid for it.

Seven

He said he'd been paying for it all his life and for a long time I believed him. Poor boy. Poor boy from a poor family housed by the Welfare. His passion was football but his talent was music and that didn't sit sweetly. Music was for girls, was for toffs, was for anyone but a son of mine, his father said, and sent him to training. He was happy to go. He was one of the boys. He was far more sportsman than musician, didn't have that artist's disposition to keep him lurking on the touchline, ridiculed because he couldn't play. He could play. He would have liked to have played in the Premiership. He would have liked to have had that certain intelligence which would let him pick a spot with his eye, then position a ball there with his foot, but the touch of magic present in his music was lacking in his football and practice didn't make perfect. His legs made sense with a cello between them.

Eight

The body of a cello, he postured once, is like the body of a woman, all curves. Maybe this was why he was so resentful of them. It wasn't the accident that produced the anger but rather the other way round. Lack of choice, he told me, irritated him. It was so unfair! He didn't want to rebel! Music marked him out.

But . . . So he liked to think, a lot of the time.

Is this the source of my discomfort: contradiction in my feeling? It was hard when he was living, harder now he's dead. I've not yet managed to forget. I've not yet managed to blank out, or feel less keenly, his idiocy. The process always turns sour; a nastiness descends. It sticks. It's on my back, it's in my throat, I feel superstitious, I need some cleansing ritual: burn this notebook, wash my clothes, cut my hair. Something wants to come out. Something wants to be started again.

Nine

Lee said, 'I've started over once, I don't think I can do it again.' I agreed with him. Now, *I* go over and over it, hoping the end might change. Even in this courtroom, watching James tell his story, I keep wishing it's not going to finish the way that I know it will. It's like going to see *Macbeth* and hoping he won't kill Duncan. It's like watching the news and hearing the punchline first, then the story, and willing the end to be anything but . . .

Could it possibly be otherwise? How far would I have to go back to alter the outcome? To that day I agreed with him? To Gina arriving and coming between them? To their meeting? My mind has become a racetrack run backwards, it stops at hurdles knocked over and tries to put them up again – if he'd done, if she'd done, (but most of all) if I'd done – in company, I'm impatient to be alone again so I can think about it all, but when alone, no one can bore me to the dismal extent that I can. I want a lobotomy. I write everything down until it's no longer interesting, until it no longer interests me, until my mind can move onto something else; but . . . Could it possibly be otherwise?

Somehow each thought is too much. I write them in these manic numbered paragraphs, the numbers being doodled while the thought consolidates. I write them down so my mind will move on and I write them down so I'll never move on, so I'll never forget a thing. It is a sad truth that you can put anybody out of mind.

Ten

Lee is tall, his legs are strong, the top half of his body flows freely, his feet support him squarely on the ground. He is made for the cello (or maybe the cello made him like this?) he is made for the ballet. His collarbone juts out distinctly, a structure from which the rest of his body seems to hang, from which the rest of his body is predictable. It is long and athletic, it is naked and proud in the forest. In public places I have often thought human beings ugly as a species. Minus their clothes with their hairless bodies and pockets of fat, their bottoms, their bellies, their saggy dugs and ancient genitalia, they are among the ugliest creatures on earth. Not Lee. He is evolved from generations running through the forest.

He is evolved from Nancy and Bob who sit in the front row. They roll cigarettes which they smoke in the recess. I'd only seen bits of them before, in the photos Lee showed me of him as a child. Their knees in the foreground, their dinners upon them, the brown carpet, the television.

Eleven

I remember how I noticed, going round to his house, that there weren't any photos of them anywhere. For some time I'd thought it was slightly affected, his reluctance to talk about them, his turning perceptibly strange and sour at their mention, but then I went to his house and, no photos. None in albums, none on walls. Lots of pictures of him, pictures pinned to a board – on holiday, in concert, pulling a stupid face – as though to remind him of who he was; but none of them, I noticed. Not anywhere.

Twelve

James's mother gets up every morning and puts her hair in rollers. She brushes it out and pins it up in a sensitive sweep from the nape of her neck. Beneath it I have seen a small thumbprint of a birthmark, often obscured by the clasp of her necklace. It must be some time, I imagine, since she's had a reason, every morning, to get up and wash her hair.

I imagine she did it anyway. That's the sort she seems. Polished. She's had five children but it doesn't show, not physically, I can see, not emotionally, I have heard. I wonder how this disaster is affecting her famous detachment. I wonder how she finds it, sitting beside her ex in his pinstripe suit, as she must have done at breakfast once. Sitting beside her offspring, part of her body once. If they recognize Lee's parents, they don't show it.

Thirteen

But I, I recognize everyone, all the major players. Putting faces to names and bodies to people whose stories I've heard is a pleasure I have recently discovered. Its thrill is quite distinct. It's a tiny stab of power. It buoys me up through these dismal days, until I remember that I'd like to tell Lee I've seen so and so and realize that I can't, I'd like to hear Lee laugh at my rendition but I can't recall, exactly, what his laugh was like, I'd like to see the passion in his face when he speaks of James or Bob, but there's no such thing as Lee's face any more, Lee's face does not exist.

Fourteen

Except in our heads, and what does he look like there! In James's, in Bob's, in Gina's, in mine; are any two the same? I see him as a boy, as a baby, as a teenager, as all those Lees I never knew. No future to be imagined now, my mind creates a past in compensation. Images of Lee like the snapshots he showed me, aged three, dressed up as Superman, aged five like a centurion, aged seven, striking some hilarious pose. I have a sense of him, but I wish I had his memories, because, how much have I invented? Even when he was alive, how much did I invent?

Fifteen

At fourteen his hair grows over his ears and he brushes it away from his brow with the tips of his fingers. His eyes are shaped like almonds and coloured granite, his nose has not yet set, his lips are cherry red. He lives in a terraced house with a yard down the side in which he kicks his football, but he's not doing so well at that these days. In his bedroom he sits cross-legged on his single bed looking out of the window over the gardens, back-to-back, side-by-side. He's popular at school. On Tuesdays and Thursdays Miss Graham gives him piano lessons in his lunch-hour. She's new, Miss Graham, she's fit, she thinks he's got talent.

He would have preferred the guitar but she captured him with her flattery, keeping him back at the end of a music lesson, telling him she'd noticed him, pointing out his sense of rhythm, saying she'd teach him for free. She told him he had perfect pitch, something he'd never heard of before, she told him he was gifted. He went at first because he was curious, he stayed because he loved the attention. It grew as his knowledge grew and he caught on surprisingly quickly. It was like, he already knew this, like someone had already taught him; he didn't have to make the effort to learn so much as remember. And then, this was something that he could do that nobody else could do, and he could do it easily.

She brought in her cello to show him, for fun more than anything else, but when he sat behind it, he said, and held it, he felt excited, he felt right. The instrument was his inside embraced by his outside, its music, his whole body presented, he could hug it in his arms, feel it in pulses between his legs, it was a dance they did together, it was an intimate act. His playing, lacking in technique, rough, was never abrasive, it had a libidinous quality which saved it, which drove it straight to the heart of that space which makes us tremble, excited, afraid, overtaken, relieved.

Sixteen

I look at James but I don't see it. I can't imagine them together. I can't imagine them best friends, intimates, in each other's pockets. I can't see them, it hurts to see them, why does it hurt to see them?

Why does it hurt to picture them together, young and careless, as they must have been at college? All that shared history that I'll never be a part of? I feel left out? I feel possessive? I know that their friendship, despite its dysfunction, was stronger than Lee's friendship with me?

But it seems all wrong in the pictures I conjure. the two of them alone together – on a Sunday, watching TV; in cahoots at somebody's party; laughing at some shared memory. This person. With *this* one? They saw each other three times a week, they spoke to each other every day. Lee, who would not be pinned down by anyone else, and – James? What was it?

Seventeen

At first they thought it was an accident, an overdose, but something didn't sit right. He'd been drunk, he'd had four or five sleeping pills, he'd taken a little cocaine, but nothing to cause such a massive explosion in his heart. And the prick of the needle they found in his arm had not, as they'd assumed at first, injected the coke – that had been snorted. So what was the needle for? And where was it now? Not in Lee's house.

Not that it was Lee's house, it was one of James's, and as everyone knew James wanted him out. They had fallen out. It was a very public disagreement. It took place in bars and at parties, it filtered through to colleagues at work, it demanded comment from mutual friends. It was huge and obsessive and desperate – the break up of a marriage – it employed foul play and dirty tricks. And then, the dirtiest trick of all.

Eighteen

James's eyes are furtive and nervous, they look like he is scheming, they are counting against him. How's the jury to know that they always look this way? They are mirrored by his father's – two identical pairs of watery eyes looking into each other, looking away. He is the image of his father. The same balding pate, the lack in the chin, how can Gina be kissed by him? When she touches his translucent skin does she think of Lee? His unexpected softness?

I have caught her looking at me, wondering whether to speak to me, wondering whether I'd speak. I wonder too. There's so much that I'd want her to say to me, more than she'd be able to tell. She lived with him. She knew him in those small things that join us together. Those daily rituals that yet are almost secrets. The weird intimacy of watching someone you know brush their teeth the first time you watch it. Would she even have noticed the things that I'd want her to tell? That drawer that I found which was filled with his personal admin ... the (almost) comfort it gave, the minutiae of another person's life. And this person! this hedonist, this Peter Pan – everything neatly stacked in folders, each folder neatly titled in his round writing: the address of the house he was living in, bank statements, payslips, bills, the financial year ... the incredible burst of fondness for him then ...

Fondness too late! Fondness that hurt. The last few weeks of his life I'd felt no fondness at all, only: *he isn't worthy of my friendship; he's moody, unreliable, he's self-absorbed; he's endlessly sensitive but only as far as himself.* I even thought I'd drop him, I thought I'd be happier if I didn't see him. How comic that seems when faced with this. This journey we make to this courtroom, this ritual, as though time has stood still, this story, the same story, over and over—

Nineteen

Michael Cabresi set up his school for strings primarily so he'd have musicians to conduct. Musicians who would, eventually, all have been trained by him. It was in its infancy still when he heard Lee playing Mahler at the top of an escalator in the Underground. *Das Klagende Leid.*

Something drew him towards it – the oddness of the cantata condensed, the flute and the oboe sung low by strings – but then he stood still. He watched this boy, his hair sweating at his temples, his long, untrained fingers. Fingers, Cabresi decided, he wanted to teach—

But his school was new, his orchestra had not yet found

its voice. He depended on tuition fees and these were high. There was no way Lee's parents could afford them. There was no way they'd want to, his father said.

Twenty

His father holds his mother's hand. He runs his thumb across the tips of her fingers. Nothing but justice and that's not enough. Nothing will bring back his son. Perhaps he goes back to the day it began, the day when he knew that he'd lost him forever, the day he came home to that man in his house, and the sound of two cellos . . .

Bob knew when he saw him that he'd get what he wanted, that he wouldn't give up, he knew exactly who he was. That man Lee had met who ran that school, he'd sent some information and written a letter. So now he'd turned up. He'd brought his cello with him. He was in Bob's front room with his wife and his son and they were playing Schumann.

Not that he knew that. This was something about which he knew nothing at all. Did that scare him?

Is that why he objected? He couldn't afford the fees but Cabresi waived them. He wouldn't allow Lee to go. But Lee was sixteen, he could leave home. The next time Cabresi came round, when he left, Lee went with him.

Does he feel vindicated? Does he feel guilty? Doesn't life always prove you right? If Lee hadn't gone to that place he'd still be alive, but if Bob hadn't protested, and protested so strongly – Lee's alienation at college and his isolation at home, his character needing to make itself, fighting to make itself known, its anger, its arrogance, the accident—

James always had it so easy. He had always been sent to the finest schools that money could buy. Much good had it done him. He wasn't academic, he wasn't sporty and he wasn't artistic, he didn't even have many friends. He wasn't bright enough to go to a good university, he hadn't the inclination to start a career, so Cabresi's school (his sister's suggestion) seemed just the ticket. He wasn't especially talented. But he played the violin passably well. He wasn't in love with music. But the school was new and his father was rich and with his son's application he enclosed a donation. His son's application was successful.

Twenty-one

It's too much to suppose that this extra finance paid for Lee's tuition but my mind's already made that connection. It can't help itself. It has to find coincidence, seek out portents of doom, there has to be no other way this could have happened, would that it were meant to be. Some people believe there's a reason for all interaction. Some people *believe* it. That every relationship is karmic, that we forever return to the arms of those we love; or hate (there's no middle ground in the game of reincarnation). How apt for this drama. No emotion is muted. Love, obsession, jealousy, revenge. Was Cabresi's attraction to Lee some recognition from a previous life? Was James's destined from beyond the grave? I wish that it were. I long to know that all of it was preordained. I don't want to think that life is all there is, and Lee is dead.

But this is what I do think.

There were eight empty cans of lager in the bin and an empty glass by the side of the sofa. Traces of Rohypnol were found in two of the cans and '*James, 7.30*' written in Lee's diary on the night that he died. A witness saw James leaving Lee's house at 9.30 that evening.

James says he wasn't leaving, he was arriving, that he hadn't been invited round till half past nine; he says when he got there, nobody answered the door. But his fingerprints are on the glass and the cans of lager, and Gina left his house at six o'clock that night to go to work, so he doesn't have an alibi, and he and Lee had fallen out.

It wasn't over her but she proved a willing ingredient. The situation was just too dynamic to leave it alone. I know. I understand. That strange connection they had, it was almost sexy. Coming between them. Blowing it to smithereens. Choose me. Choose me over him.

Lee was addictive. He was warm and attractive and passionate, he was full. There were so many things you'd imagine he'd be, so much at his disposal. He hooked Gina as he hooked me, just as all those years ago he hooked Cabresi. Cabresi couldn't resist him. The romance of him, the pygmalion fantasy, the father who stood in his way, that beaten-up cello. His whole body was a cello, Lee told him, strings ran down his middle, through his heart, he could feel them quiver; the cello can break your heart, the way it seems to cry, to implore. It broke Lee's when he started college, funded by Cabresi, shunned by Bob (and again when he couldn't play it any more), but it wasn't meant to be like this.

This wasn't Cabresi's intention. Things got out of hand

the way they always did with Lee. He wanted to teach the boy, not rip him from his family, not house him, clothe him, feed him, this wasn't how it started.

Twenty-two

How did it start then? When? With *Das Klagende Leid*? Or years earlier perhaps, when Cabresi was a similar age, younger, found by a similar teacher, who taught him now for a cut of his earnings later, who taught him everything he knew? Did Cabresi hope history might repeat itself? He couldn't put Lee out of his mind. He went several times to the spot where Lee busked, talked to him, coached him, flattered him; he told him about his school. Lee was unconvinced – not that he didn't want to go, he was going to teach PE – but Cabresi kept up his patter: the musical life, a noble life, the thrill of performance, the communion with old masters. Once Lee was seduced, he sent his father a letter.

He heard nothing. Worse, Lee had disappeared. Why? He didn't understand. For someone so ill-educated musically this was an amazing opportunity. He'd have to pay a visit. He had to find out why. He took his cello – like some suit of armour – and he caught a train. What did he have to lose?

He checked his motives during the journey. Why this sudden, overwhelming interest in a boy of sixteen? He couldn't explain. Lee wasn't the most talented musician he'd ever encountered, but there *was* something in his playing, an almost sexual thing. Anger, passion, energy, sex, they were the same, integral, unteachable, the difference between a good player and a great one. This was what he told himself as the train made its way to Lee's part of town. He had chanced upon a wonderful potential. He hated to see it going to waste.

Nancy was at home with Lee when Cabresi arrived and flattered his way into their house. There was pride in her eyes while Lee and Cabresi played but her expression changed abruptly the moment Bob came in. Yes, he knew of Cabresi's school, Lee had told him all about it, but he couldn't afford those fees, and even if he could – what was Cabresi doing putting ideas like this in a young boy's head? The trouble he'd caused, the tantrums they'd had, hadn't they, Nancy? Yes echoed Nancy, it was all very well, but—

But Cabresi was swept up in fantasy all the way home. He was going to get that boy. He was going to turn him into the finest cellist the world had ever known.

He didn't have their number so he had to pay a second visit but he was glad of that. What he had to say he wanted to say in person, he wanted to see their faces. He made the journey with a mounting excitement, imagining the scene about to unfold. Nancy opening the door perhaps, surprised to see him. Bob being brusque at first then gradually warming. Lee falling to his knees (no, he wouldn't do that), Lee jumping up with a youthful exuberance. The whole family embracing him warmly.

He'd spent all week with his accountant doing the sums. His school was highly subscribed that year, he'd received a hefty donation from one of his patrons, his ensemble was getting more and more bookings – he could afford it. Sure there was ground to make up, but he knew Lee could do it. A little hard work and determination. A bit of encouragement from the maestro himself. Nothing could have prepared him for his reception, he was barely allowed through the door. His generous speech failed in the face of such antagonism, the words 'accountant', 'free place' and 'wonderful talent' falling out of his mouth in a disjointed jumble. 'I've told you,' said Bob, 'it's not what we want for our son.'

He walked away unable to think for some minutes. He paused at the end of the street to catch his breath. What was Bob's objection? he wondered. How could he do this to his son? 'Maybe he mistrusts my motives,' he thought, 'maybe he's right to.' He felt a little sick and a little disgusting, as though his whole being had been shot to pieces and not just his fantasy of the past few days. In ten minutes' time, he consoled himself, he'd be on the train and this episode would pass away with the scenery. He'd never see Bob again. Or Nancy. Or Lee. His life would go on with nothing to do with theirs.

He wanted to be gone as quickly as possible and was angry he'd just missed a train. He walked down the platform slowly to kill the time, then sat on a bench and stared into space. When he focused it was on a figure carrying a bag and what looked like a cello. It was a cello. It was Lee. 'I've left,' he said, 'I'm sixteen, it's allowed.' He said it defiantly, waiting for Cabresi's response but there was none. 'I want to go to your school.'

'Go home.'

'No,' said Lee, 'I can't. You don't understand. There's

been a row,' and then, 'It's your fault. You've got to take me with you.' And Cabresi, the puff gone out of him, didn't put up a fight.

Twenty-three

'I was only sixteen,' he says to me, 'and my parents stopped speaking to me. Dad said, "You've made your choice". This was a chance for me, he didn't get that. Things like this don't happen to boys like me. But I could have forgiven him – he'd made his feelings clear right from the start – it was her I couldn't forgive.'

'Nancy?'

'Yes.' I hold my breath. I wait for him. He doesn't usually talk about them, shrugs them off if I mention them, changes the subject. But, 'She loved me to perform – I'll show you photos. She dressed me up, made me pose . . . Anyway. Whatever she thought she always stuck by him. It was always me against the two of them. I hated her for that.'

'Do you hate her now?'

'. . . It's difficult – she defers to him the whole time. It's the way she makes it work.'

'Their relationship?'

'Yes.'

'But it works.'

'I suppose. They're a unit.'

'Did you find it exclusive?'

'Sometimes.'

'Were you lonely?'

'I thought I was until I left. Imagine what it's like,

living with the maestro. Sixteen years old. Knowing he hadn't meant it to happen. Seeing your "talent" through his eyes now, now that he has to clean up after you, share his bachelor space with you, find your hairs in his bath. Somehow you find yourself here. Somehow events have all turned out like this. You've got to make it work. You've got to practise and practise and please him and be as good as he believed you'd be because you know he's wondering if he made the right decision. But you're frightened and lonely and angry. And then the term starts.'

Twenty-four

This is the point to which my mind returns. This is the point to which it sticks. A moment in time which isn't my own, regrets for a past from which I am absent. This much isn't my fault. This much can be blamed on Bob, on Cabresi, on cause and effect. Imagine a boy, sixteen years old, living with a stranger in a strange world – and then the term starts. There were others, more accomplished, who weren't being tutored for free, it made Lee's teachers uncomfortable, their discomfort made them cruel. Often, in front of the class, they would pick him up on some point of technique he hadn't yet mastered and make him repeat it, repeat it, repeat it! while everyone waited; everyone who knew where he lived and thought this cause to avoid him. What did he have to fall back on? Not his talent, not his patron's affection, not words of kindness from his peers, no, he was ostracized, something of a curiosity, at night he left with Cabresi while the others went home. And then there was James.

James was a lifestyle, a habit, something Lee grew into. Could it ever have been otherwise? Was it purely circumstantial or was it the decisions he made? The decisions he made so long before that he couldn't remember, but which set the pattern. I am Lee. This is what I do. No way to undo that pattern.

But it happens like that, so snugly, life gives you just what you don't need. It knows how predictable you are, it robs you of choice. If there hadn't been a James in his class, what then? But there was a James in his class. They met each other's requirements exactly.

So, I am not in charge. It is not my fault. Lives have a momentum of their own. This one was never my responsibility – this play was in act three before I took the stage! (But I took the stage; I egged him on; I filled his head with my ideas.) Cabresi had found him, he thought he'd feel confident, that the others would respect him. But he felt intimidated where they had a nonchalance, it was an alien world to him. *His* father had never played Chopin in the evenings, or smugly put on Mozart in the car. He didn't *own* the music. He handled it with almost a reverence, as a thing quite outside of him, something he found confusing, then frightening, and then overwhelming. It was a wonderful thing to hear.

Not that I heard it. Not that I ever heard it. This early life must be, for the most part, imagined, and not just by me. The stories he told me, the versions I've heard in this courtroom, a slight difference here, a slight difference there, but always this outcome. Wishing the outcome would change. He was something of a lonely protégé until he met

James. Mediocre James who, even now in Prada, looks like a geek. Giftless James, undistinguished, unexceptional, nothing to write home about, no great shakes, was a cipher. He wore the right clothes, the right accent and the right kind of family, he gave Lee a passport; and Lee, with his talent, his football scarf and his third-hand cello that nobody helped him to buy, gave James glamour. This, they called friendship.

Twenty-five

But when he needed him most, Lee had to admit, James was there. The accident did not just kill his career, it killed his confidence. It was the shame of it. Not only what happened that night but what wasn't to happen as a result. The live wire had blown himself up. He'd been going to be the best. He had to be. To spite his parents, to excuse his arrogance, to explain his outlandish behaviour. He developed a fear of all those he'd been rude to, sneered at, blanked, the ones who'd been waiting to watch him fall. He imagined them everywhere. He couldn't go out. He felt like he had no skin. James used to go round and sit with him. Demanding nothing, offering nothing, watching TV. And when he did go out again, eventually, James was always with him.

Twenty-six

'These fingers,' he says to me, holding up his left hand, the last two digits jutting towards me, 'these were all I had.

Took much more than that for me to play, but that was all it took to stop me. Doesn't seem fair.'

He grins, his childlike rage at the injustice of the world is a joke we share – but it doesn't seem fair. There's that squeeze in my stomach, this time like guilt: I was impatient with him, inconsiderate of how hard it had been, I only saw my own expectations not being met; I never cut him any slack.

But how much slack did he ever cut anybody? 'Don't judge me' was his favourite thing to say, even when one wasn't. Yet he, he challenged everyone, at every opportunity and his purpose was not always to speak as he found, but to wound. He saw them as explosions of truth, these character attacks, but he used the truth like a sword, 'I'm just telling you the truth!' 'I'm only saying what I see' 'You do this thing' 'This is what you do' 'This is what you're like'.

Once someone defines you, it's hard to prove them wrong, as though their expectations are stronger than your actions, as though the dark side looms larger the moment it gets some attention, because no motive can ever be completely pure. Cabresi was manipulative, Gina was passive-aggressive, I didn't care; it was destructive, his take on the world. He was self-destructive, he was generally destructive, in the end, he was destroyed.

Twenty-seven

It was presented so matter-of-factly by the coroner. As if this wasn't a human being who'd died but some machine, packed in. Some spanner in the works led this part to malfunction which in turn sparked off reactions here and here; a series of explosions, a starvation of air, no way to repair the damage, all systems shut down. The technical side of this story. The end at the beginning. The coroner standing up first to present the conclusion, then the bit-part players in the drama to show how it got there, to give its emotional side.

This is how he died, said the coroner.

This is how he died, suggested the testimonies of everyone else.

Is this how he died? At the hands of *him*? The last to take the stand?

Those same hands grip the rail in front of him or stray abstractedly into his mouth. He doesn't bite his nails, just cleans them on his canines, or sucks the tip of a finger between his teeth. I hate this man. It is stronger than hate, it is disgust. A clammy finger in a rosebud mouth, they're too red, his lips, too Cupid's bow. His eyes are blue and blank and blinking. His hair is cut close. His scalp becomes skin in patches by his temples, joining in an arc and leaving stranded an island of skin-coloured hair. The same colour everywhere and then that blank, blue stare, that rose-red mouth.

How long since I've hated him? How long since I turned that hatred into disgust? The first time I saw him, did I find him this repulsive physically? Would I have done so anyway, or was I predisposed to? Because I loathed him long before I met him. Reading between the lines of the stories Lee told me.

Twenty-eight

'The first time I took cocaine,' he says to me, 'was about a month after I met Lizzie. James bought it. Well – he could afford to. It was a Friday afternoon and we were going out later. We always go out on a Friday night, it's like our ritual. But I was quite into Lizzie then, I wanted to be with her, we were at that stage, you know, I couldn't be arsed with a blokes' night out.

'So James came round in the afternoon, which was odd because he never came round. I still lived with Cabresi then and he didn't like James and James knew. He shot off into my bedroom and put on the cricket and we lounged around watching it. I said I didn't feel like going out and he said neither did he – shame because he'd got some coke. But I wanted to try it. I said, maybe we should just stay in and do a line and he made some joke, like, how it would be funny, watching cricket, feeling manic—

'Nothing major happened, I was just on form, suddenly happy, suddenly sharp; suddenly, completely in the mood for a beer, a beer would be fantastic. So off we went and had one and one became two and three and a bit more coke and down some club and a couple of Es and I didn't see Lizzie that night, I didn't see her that whole weekend. And afterwards, if we ever didn't feel like going out we'd do a line,' he winks at me. 'Get us in the mood . . .'

That's the Lee that I hate, with that twinkle in his eye. That drug twinkle. Wickedness. Fun. I never thought we were the same, no, but there was a path, there was a core, there was an understanding. Not when he had that twinkle in his eye.

Then, there was another life, another world that I didn't have access to, a sensation I'd never experience, had no desire to. Suddenly, cleanly, a breaking of the ways, *I am not you.* All the progress we'd made . . .

This story comes through me as though it were mine. It is. It's the way that I make sense. To tell it to myself, to understand it, to store it within me, two histories in one body because his body's gone.

But now that his body's gone, now that I think about his dead life more than I think about my own, now that it's hard to tell which one's alive and which one's not, I view it all so clearly. I get it. I don't take it personally. See how the child learns, see how he learns. Watch as the dog jumps through the hoop.

Twenty-nine

He was a late starter, he was conscious of that, he had to work harder than everyone else. He did work harder – but it didn't pay off. How could he hear how it was supposed to sound, see in his mind how to produce the sound, but not command his fingers to make the sound? Why was it so hard for him?

He was in prison, he realized, he didn't want to be here but he couldn't go back, he had to be *some* good. But the world had grown much vaster suddenly. He wasn't at school any more with Miss Graham. He wasn't the best in his class. He wasn't only here, next to Cabresi, next to his peers who'd been playing for long years before him; he also took his place in a line of musicians living and dead. Who was he among them?

The injustice of it all came clearer to him the more he went on practising, the later it grew, the next time Cabresi shouted at him. If he wasn't going to be much good why did his talent have to be music, might as well have been football – at least then he'd still be at home. At home! With Nancy and Bob who'd made him alone. The others here, they didn't know they were born. That easy confidence that only money could buy, the chances they'd had, the things they'd known. He'd work himself up to a fury. Knees trembling, fingers pressed hard against the strings, bow angrily sweeping out notes, pitying himself, hating this life, robbed of all choice. And just as he was feeling most furious Cabresi would yell out 'That's it'.

Thirty

'I was yelling at them, I was shouting, "You're all such wankers. Look at you in your expensive suits, in your flash bar with your fat wallets in your pockets. You're such smug bastards. You're pathetic." James was loving it. He loved it when I behaved like that. Being outrageous. Pissing everyone off. He never had the guts to do it himself. He'd say, "I've left you a line in the toilet," and I'd go and take it. Like medicine. Like my reward. That's if we didn't get chucked out first.'

Thirty-one

Michael Cabresi is fifty-six, young, but he doesn't look it. It isn't just his greyed hair or dulled skin but a thickness round his bones. He moves as though inside himself, carrying his flesh like a winter coat, stiff under its weight, hardened by this cold. I'd never seen him so close before, never walking like a man in a room, only onto a stage, upon a podium, taking up his baton as a different physical being, one made light, his arms like wings riding the music. I have seen this man conduct. I have seen him in grand auditoriums and church crypts, I have seen him in draughty halls. I once saw him conduct a young orchestra in a room so small that seats had been crammed behind the musicians. I could see his face, could see its changing passions, progenitive agony, frustration and delight.

Here, he placed a hand on a Bible, simply a hand, slightly swollen, slightly petrified. I watched him. Inside his head, memories to match the stories Lee told me, stories I've replayed to get a purchase on my friend, stories from which I am excluded, of which jealous. Let me hear them. I never thought I'd hear them from you.

I never thought I'd get the opportunity – who would? Not just talking with you, Michael, about him, that would be something in itself, but hearing you interrogated, forced to tell the truth, the whole truth, nothing but the truth.

He sat down. He waited. It seemed a long time coming, the first question, and then questions rolled away so it appeared to me his was a narrative uninterrupted, the Lee he presented, man and boy, the boy in his house, the boy's friend . . .

The boy in his house is shy and proud, moody and eager to please, self-absorbed and generous. Easily enraged but this much is good, this much can be turned to musical advantage. He seems to respond when the odds are stacked against him, the source of his passion is anger, the awareness of the situation he is in. His general life situation, his social class, his parents, the cello, the place he now lives, the place he studies, the way they treat him here, the impossibility of what is expected, the lateness of his age in starting serious training. At first being a late starter makes him want to work harder than everyone else but after a while it just makes him act up. If he can't be the best musician he'll have the biggest personality.

Personality is what's important to his friend, the bigger the better, the louder the better, it's what he counts as cred. Lee has all those things that make him angry, all those things against him, on his side, they mark him out as different. This isn't the life he'd been expecting to lead, this isn't the point he'd been working to reach, he's been discovered, patronized, he lives with Cabresi and no one's sure why, he's good but he isn't great, there's mystery about him, no one can quite get a hook on him. He just needs someone to point this all out, to make a fuss of him, to make him feel special, little orphan boy. It's bad luck this someone turns out to be James.

James isn't good news but Cabresi feels he may be biased. It riles him to have to admit students like that, rich but no good, to keep his business afloat. And if there seems to be something about this particular student, something spooky, the way he slinks round corners, moves noiselessly down corridors, you turn around and there he is, suddenly appearing, always looking like he's up to something, perhaps it's just Cabresi's prejudice.

Besides, he's glad that Lee has made a friend at last. Besides, he isn't Lee's father, what can he do? He should have left him with his father.

There's been no contact with the parents though Cabresi has tried, persuaded Lee to phone, to write, but he's given up because of that look on Lee's face when he gets no response, or Bob barking 'You've made your choice' or Nancy sounding pleased, then scared, then replacing the receiver. How can they do this? Cabresi doesn't have children so he has no idea but he feels he should have left him there. Here Lee's lonely, he doesn't fit in; there he's ostracized.

And he's only sixteen. It's hard enough, he remembers, working out who you are, making yourself, without this resentment, this solitude, this insecurity. This is where James sneaks in.

He says 'sneaks' with hindsight. He says it now that he knows that there's nothing spontaneous, nothing artless about this person. Looking back, he bides his time, he picks his moment, he leaves it a couple of months while Lee is the odd one out, the frequent topic of conversation, and then he begins to befriend him. From out of nowhere he invites Lee home for Christmas; when term starts again they're as thick as ten snakes. He's three years older than Lee, it's hardly an equal relationship. It's a scheme he's concocted, some way to get in to mark himself as 'someone', which his talent wouldn't, to get himself a ticket to the party, which his personality couldn't, it's not born of genuine kindness or interest. Anyone else and things might have been different. Anyone else and Lee might have joined in; James hives him away, his friend only. And then, a subtle shift in Lee's personality, so slight as to be barely noticed: shyness that kept him apart from his peers is replaced by resentment for what they've got, anger for not befriending him, uncertainty gives way to conceit. They become the odd couple. Exclusive, eccentric. James gains notoriety (which he never would have got by himself) and he gains Lee's dependence. Because, for Lee, what's on the other side of the friendship?

Thirty-two

'Do you see how he got me?' he says. 'Do you see how he did it?' but he has no need to point it out. It's the moment I've been waiting for, the penny dropping, understanding. Do you know how hard it is? To listen to someone you love and not to give an opinion? To wait for them to come to their own conclusion? 'Do you see how he got me?' he says, like no one but him has worked it out.

Thirty-three

One thing about James, he has a beautiful voice. There's a quality to it, warm like sing-song, reassuring like somebody reading a story. Well, he made a living from it when music failed to provide one, before he didn't need to work for his income any more. I can imagine it convincing me if I closed my eyes, if it said what I wanted to hear.

If he said I was better than the rest and I had to believe it I would. I wouldn't dream that he'd say to the rest that I'd never make it. Fuel the fire of suspicion surrounding Cabresi's patronage. Speak knowingly of my brusque personality – a personality his encouragement has helped to promote. I wouldn't see that he isolated me, yet he used me as a bridge to the others. I wouldn't ... But wouldn't I?

Frustrating, Lee's blindness. I try to understand and I do almost. But by the time we're friends he's had proof over and over again, yet still he goes back, he goes back for more. What can I say? As soon as I give an opinion this struggle with James will be mine, and it isn't, it's Lee's. It becomes my struggle anyway.

Thirty-four

But the way people fight for him. Cabresi, Lizzie, Gina, me. Our battles with James begin altruistic – it's a strange connection they have, it has a negative charge – but always take on a more personal tone: choose me! choose me over him ... Something about Lee is utterly involving. The stories he tells, or the way that he tells them, somehow your opinion becomes a conviction, something that makes you excitable, makes you embroiled. Look what Cabresi did, look what happened to Lizzie, look at Gina, still so entangled she's with his best friend. Why? What is it? Why this hideous, strong feeling? Just working it out is enough to turn you mad. Do I love him? Is it something in me? Or in him? The way people fight for him. The way he makes them.

Thirty-five

Cabresi interprets the ardour he feels as paternal. Suddenly, in his forties, he's a parent to a teenage boy with an inappropriate friend. It would be simpler, perhaps, if the ill-effects were obvious but they aren't, they're subtle, so subtle as to make him wonder if he's paranoid. James seems to be playing one side off against the other, but surely no one could be so clumsily contrived: telling Lee what the others say about him, telling those others that Lee doesn't like them, widening the gap; Cabresi sees it but he doesn't quite believe it.

What he believes is that Lee is special, extraordinary. It isn't just his physical beauty – the shape of his eyes, the line of his body, the presence of him, everything in precise proportion – but also his fire, his energy. Someone like Lee shouldn't be friends with someone like James; the discrepancy between the two of them upsets Cabresi. But it's an elitism he can't quite justify. James is far from inspirational, but is he nasty? Perhaps he sees the worst in him simply to excuse this snobbery. Certainly, though, by degrees and under James's influence, Lee replaces loneliness with bitterness, insecurity with arrogance, becomes spiteful, judgmental, has a puffed-up sense of his own importance . . .

There's a quality to Lee that makes him easy to ignite.

The result of all that's happened lately, his odd sense of justice, a latent passion evident in his music, in his sudden enthusiasm, these things can be twisted and James seems to egg him on, to stoke the embers that then erupt as rage in class or tantrum in rehearsal; congratulates him, imbues him with false confidence, fills his head with mad ideas—

But isn't this what Bob accused Cabresi of at the start of this whole mess? And doesn't he know which buttons to press, and doesn't he press them to get Lee to react, to rise, to push the anger into his bow and sweep it through his cello? Which one of them, then, is having the worst effect?

Besides, the situation's delicate. He knows about reverse psychology, doesn't want to set himself up as the enemy, give James even more of a pull. In any case, he can't stop them meeting, they're in the same school, he can't expel James, his father's a patron; the problem constantly occupies him, makes him grateful he's never had children. The lack of control, that's what frustrates him, the inability to direct a person.

Small things make him realize that James is malign. Hints he dismisses as nonsense at first. Lee feels like a misfit. James stresses it. Makes *just* the odd comment – the *rarest* reference to Lee's family, or something *just slightly* salacious about Cabresi – all while appearing to remain on-side, smiling and encouraging him. He has a pattern. He flatters Lee, compares him favourably with everyone else, boosts him up, offers undivided attention, then stops suddenly, suddenly backtracks, makes Lee work.

It's some sort of insurance. As though he knows that Lee's the beautiful one, the powerful one, the magnet, that the day will come when Lee will know it too. Most of Lee's confidence is in James's hands (because, apart from Cabresi, who else does he have?) so what he gives he then takes away; and Lee, horribly predictably, does everything he can to get it back again. Like some performing monkey! An artist needs to be his own man and he isn't, he's James's. And then his music starts to suffer.

Thirty-six

'He'd go into these moods,' he says to me. 'Completely silent. Completely for no reason whatsoever. He'd be all right with everyone else, but not with me. I'd find him joking with some bloke who I knew didn't like me and he'd just go "hi" really casually as I walked by. I hated it. I thought, Any minute now I'll have no friends at all, but he always came round. He'd say "You're quite possessive, aren't you?" if I mentioned it, but it's hard not to be possessive when you've only got one friend. I had Cabresi, but he liked me for my music, he didn't care what kind of person I was. It was always practise, practise, practise with him. If I did it, he was pleased with me, if I didn't, he wasn't, it didn't have anything to do with my personality. And Cabresi hated James. Because if I hadn't had James he could have had me one hundred per cent. When James went funny I worked harder, well, I didn't have anything else to do. When James went funny Cabresi and I got on like a house on fire, but he always came round. Give him a couple of days, he always came round.'

Thirty-seven

It was a battle fought on the sly. The two of them caught up in a pull-me-push-you with Lee in the middle. It's manageable, but then Lee's music begins to suffer. *This* is the reason he's here. *This* is what all this mess has been about. Cabresi owes it to himself, to Lee, to Bob and Nancy, it can't have been for nothing, that massive disruption. That's why he decides to do what he does. It's a risky strategy but he can't think of anything else. Lee's just turned eighteen. He's been here a year and a half. He's only part way through the studies he was late in starting but he can't think of anything else. He's not nearly ready. He'll be the youngest musician and the least proficient. It could heighten his cocksure arrogance or worsen his insecurity. But nevertheless he does it. He doesn't know how else to play it. He does it because what else can he do? Lee's just turned eighteen. Now, James has an extra pull.

Nightclubs, parties, bars . . . James has the cash and Lee has the gab: he sneaks off, stays out, comes drunk to class. All energy reserved for playing the cello is now channelled into living large, getting laid, becoming the life and the soul. Perhaps James does it on purpose. After all, wouldn't it be in his best interest if Lee didn't make it? It mustn't continue. It's stopping Lee fulfilling his potential. That's why Cabresi decides.

Thirty-eight

James is saying, 'It's nonsense. It wasn't like that. We were just two kids.'

'According to Michael Cabresi—'

'It's in his head, the whole lot of it. We went out and got trashed. That's what young men do. Jesus!'

'According to Michael Cabresi your influence was purposefully malign.'

'No.'

'Purposefully problematic.'

'You want to know what the problem was? Lee was my best friend; we were close. That's what stuck in Cabresi's throat.'

'He was jealous?'

'Yes.'

'He went to these lengths through *jealousy*?'

'He wanted Lee utterly. Lee was his little social experiment. He wanted to control him – and he couldn't. I thought at the time it was rather suspicious. There was no way Lee was good enough, he should never have done it. All this might not have happened if he hadn't.'

Another of those moments, a place to stop the clock at.

Thirty-nine

The story of Lee is that of the clashes that went on around him, that lurched him to disaster, that is its tragedy. Cabresi took Lee out of college and gave him a job in his orchestra. If he'd finished the course, been ready, been confident in his ability, perhaps he'd still be alive, perhaps he'd be playing the cello. But Cabresi took him from James because he didn't approve of Lee's friendship with James, because it didn't suit his purpose. Didn't he have an agenda? Wasn't he a tactician, his motives rarely altruistic? Then why do I blame James so much and not blame Cabresi? I don't have an answer to that.

Except that we were the same, Cabresi and I; all of us in this stand-off with James were the same. We wanted the best, James wanted the worst, that's how it started. He used nightclubs and parties and girls, he used drugs and we saw it. Lee didn't notice. So full of potential. So generous and talented and James held him back. James was malicious, that's how it started. But it became something else, personal, imperative, Cabresi felt the same.

I was relieved to hear him say so when he gave his account of Lee's friendship with James. He dressed it up, of course, in reasons you could understand if you hadn't been inside it. But I had, and I knew what he meant. He graduated Lee, far too early, he put him in the orchestra and under pressure; he hoped the thrill of performance would replace the buzz of going out. And James *was* sidelined, for months. All those concerts and rehearsals, all that ground to make up. He gave Lee a concerto just as his vigour wore out. Boccherini's Concerto in D.

Forty

'Cabresi sent my parents a programme,' he says to me, 'I knew nothing about it. It had been over two years, a long time when you're that age. I'd last seen them when I was sixteen and now I was nearly nineteen, I wasn't a boy, I wasn't the same Lee. They turned up backstage afterwards and I was nice to them, confident, not angry. It was all, "hi, good to see you", like it had been yesterday. It was so much more effective. This is my world now, and I'm strong in it, and you're not part of it.

'That night brought everything together. Everything I'd done since I'd last seen Bob and Nancy, since I followed Cabresi to the station, since I'd changed my life. The past year especially, that had been a baptism of fire, playing in the orchestra, coming up to scratch, proving myself, it was like starting college all over again. More intense though. I was actually performing. It was real life.

'I had to get it right, I had to, and that was all I thought about. All I did was play. I hardly saw James. We went our separate ways for a while. I spent twenty-four hours a day with Cabresi and he never let up. Everything revolved around the practice. Everything required my total concentration.

'He was my coach. He was my torturer. He exhausted me, emotionally, physically. He could make me feel – whatever he wanted me to feel, whatever was needed, wind me up or boost me up or reduce me to tears. Constantly, in the back of my mind, would I let the others down? Let him down? What would happen if he had to let me go? It was a job now.

'Giving me the Boccherini was a sign of his confidence in me, that spurred me, but it terrified me too. I was only just starting to find my feet. Now this. My first solo performance.

'James came. James brought Lara. I completely fell for Lara. Maybe it was just the high I had that night, I don't know. The next few months it was nothing but Lara. I was burnt out, I needed something in my head that wasn't music. And it was her.

'I had a bit more time then, you see. So whenever I could I went out with James and he'd try to get her along, and sometimes she came. We always got on, there was always a spark, but it was sexy more than romantic. She was the one in control. We slept together off and on, but it never went any further than sex. It was a six year one night stand.

'Those first few times, though, I was so pleased with myself. It was amazing the effect it had. I'd be buzzing for days. Nothing could touch me. Even Cabresi couldn't get to me. Perhaps that's why I liked her so much. Yeah, that was the best thing about it.'

Forty-one

He'd been making Lee practise Vivaldi's Concerto in G minor for two cellos. Ad infinitum. Chopping it up into sections so Lee had no notion of the whole.

'No! That phrase should sound like this . . . Do it again . . . No, do it again . . . No, again . . . Again.'

'I've got it.'

'I'll tell you when you've got it. Again. No! You're killing it. Again. Again. Again!'

Lee did do it again, but with a smile on his face, not

choking back anger, not with a thumping in his throat, not fervently, in the last throes of some terrible agony before that final moment of calm.

Perhaps Cabresi had noticed this. Perhaps Lizzie was part of some plan.

She was new in the orchestra. A few years older than Lee. Some might say a more proficient musician. She'd been there a couple of weeks but Lee didn't pay her any attention until they were made to play together; made to sit next to each other, knees practically touching. She was wearing a small summer dress which she hitched up, opened her legs, positioned her cello there. It looked incongruous, like a child smoking a cigarette, that massive instrument, her tiny frame, her delicate blonde hair, Lee nearly laughed; but then they started playing.

For him it was a focusing, a honing-in, for her it was expansion. He pushed himself into the cello, she made the cello part of her. Suddenly it became real to him that each section was named a movement; a moment of understanding. He'd never heard this piece in its entirety before. First those down-sliding minor scales: something ominous and terrific – mania – a chaotic mix of confrontation, unification; then the slow central largo: the snake-dance each cello weaves around the other, their unusually serious dialogue, sad, foreboding, longing; and then the allegro, vaguely hysterical, almost mad the phrases are, they go too far—

Completely overtaking. Completely prophetic of their fated relationship. Hiding in its notes the scar on her face, his broken fingers.

Forty-two

'When I played,' he says to me, 'I saw dancers in my head. I'd think, In my next life I'm going to be a dancer. I'm going to dance a pas de deux to Tchaikovsky's *Rococo Variations* – the andante – the woman the oboe, the cello the man. I could see it. I could stretch it. I was finished when I couldn't play. I was nothing. I had nothing. People thought James was my best friend, he wasn't, it was my cello. It sounds pretentious to say. You won't understand it if you've never had anything like it. It's yours. It defines you. It is you.'

Forty-three

After the accident he developed a fear of going outside. At first this was mental – in some way rational: he didn't want to bump into Lara or Lizzie or anyone he associated with them. And by quick degrees, the terror of seeing Lara or Lizzie became the terror of seeing anyone. It was a surprisingly – shockingly – short step. He couldn't let anyone see him! He couldn't go outside.

Willingly his body responded to his mind. It gave him a means to justify his paranoia. In this way there was one less thing he could hate himself for. He felt he had started to calcify, as though there was a thread running from his knees to his shoulders that by steady degrees was being pulled taut. His muscles constricted. There was no air in him, no room. He couldn't pull himself free from himself; he had to tell himself to breathe. Inside, moving from one room to another, he hardly noticed how slowly he walked, but outside, he couldn't cross the road before the green man went red. It really *was* embarrassing to be seen walking as slowly and as purposefully as an arthritic, it really *was* awkward to go into shops when his hand trembled like a junky's, counting out change. Everybody *was* out to get him, jostling him aside in the corridors of the Tube, stealing the seat he desperately needed.

Forty-four

He wouldn't have believed it if you'd told him, if you'd held up a picture of the future while he played Vivaldi with Lizzie he would not have believed it. How far he'd come in seven short years. How much he'd lose. Lizzie his lover, Cabresi his father, the orchestra his family. But his ego, and his huge insecurity. That feeling of never being quite good enough. He hates that feeling, it makes him angry. That fire that is so necessary in his music often erupts. And James bides his time, he picks his moment. He's always on hand to stir things up when Lee's feeling down, when he's fallen out with Cabresi, or had another argument with Lizzie.

Then, suddenly, he's got something to prove, a score to settle, suddenly no longer accepts that others are chosen to solo, or that other pieces featuring other string instruments are just as important to play. It's as though a storm is constantly rising, then breaking, Cabresi placates him, makes some concession, but those periods of calm become shorter, the rages closer and closer together. It shouldn't surprise him that one day history repeats itself. That one day he packs his bags and leaves, leaves home, that he and Cabresi don't speak. It's eerily in keeping that when he tries to make contact Cabresi doesn't reciprocate. But that was twelve months later, just after the accident, Lizzie was in the ensemble. To Cabresi it was a question of loyalty. He felt he *couldn't* return Lee's calls.

Forty-five

James is saying, 'It wasn't just Cabresi who didn't take his calls, it was all of them. It was every musician he'd ever known – it was his whole community. I was the only one who stuck by him. I turned out to be his only friend.'

But the Prosecution reflects that friendship back to him: 'Controlling, obsessive and jealous.'

James shakes his head.

'You reeled him in when he was vulnerable.'

'No.'

'When he was new and alone at the school you both went to, when his heart was broken by his girlfriend . . . When his fingers were broken and his career was over.'

'It wasn't like that.'

'You manipulated situations to make him your friend.'

'I didn't.'

'You didn't like it when he got back on his feet.'

'I helped him get back on his feet.'

'You tried to bring him down. So you could be the one to pick him up.'

'No.'

'So he'd be indebted to you.'

'Not at all.'

But he did. And if Lee hadn't died James would have done it again.

Forty-six

Is it true, though, can it be true, was James really so calculating? You know of them, you've read of them, but do they actually exist, people like this? Noting our vulnerability, using it as a means to get in, their eyes on the main chance, waiting to watch us fall. Are they real or just a construct? A focus for our paranoia? I hardly believe in them and yet – Lee is dead.

Forty-seven

I remember a line from William Burroughs: *If air bubbles could kill you there wouldn't be a junky alive.* Not if you push in enough air. Not if you push it in hard. For that, your victim must be willing or unconscious. James would have knelt on Lee's arm, knees either side of his elbow joint, elbow pressed into the ground, the soft skin where Lee's arm bends, stretched, those two veins underneath it juicy and fat, the needle goes in, a syringe full of air pumped with the force of his body; a pause, a wait for the bubble to reach his heart – how long will it take? a minute? five? ten? If it goes to his lungs or his brain it won't necessarily kill him; he might have to go through the process again. Can he face it? A convulsion. Panic in Lee's body. A seizure. A fit. A horrible gasping for life. But small display for what's been extinguished. All that, those years, those loves, those ideas, those lives touched, those moments of despair; this stillness, quiet, calm. I see how he lay there. In my mind, I see how he lay.

Forty-eight

But I see him everywhere. In the backs of heads that are vaguely similar, in the flash of a profile, his features arrange before my eyes have adjusted. When he was alive it was the same, only now I encourage it. Then it just gave a dull stab of pain because I knew that he didn't see me.

He was some sort of drug for me. Seeing him would make me elated, buoyed up, hopeful, positive, benign. But the feeling would dissipate. He'd disappoint mc, hc'd say something mean, he wouldn't turn up. That connection I'd felt, that connection with him, would vanish, my connection with the world; nothing to hold on to, no headway made with anybody, you live your life I live mine, it's illusion that we don't all stand alone. It was like withdrawal, total and painful and solitary, and then it would pass. My life would resume an anodyne normality. And then I'd see him, and the whole horrid process started again. Didn't it hurt just as much when he was alive? But now he's dead and there's no end to this cold turkey. I keep him alive in the pages of this notebook.

Forty-nine

He would often shout at me, 'Why was it music, not football?' – there could be an almost idiotic rage inside him. It would burst forth abruptly, brought on by drink sometimes, by drugs, by the recollection of an incident he found unjust. I ventured once that he was lucky it was anything at all and he went for me. What did I know with my mediocre life? Had I ever excelled at anything? He doubted it. But lucky me. He longed to be that ordinary.

He was so arrogant. He was so angry. He would turn so suddenly.

Like playing with a lion, beautiful and magnificent and cuddly, but the sharpness of his teeth – almost sexy. I feel safe beside you against the rest of the world but I don't quite trust you not to hurt me. (And neither should I, for look what happened to Lizzie.) And underneath it all, that amazing vulnerability.

Fifty

Lizzie said, 'He was nineteen, I was twenty-one. I never thought it would last for seven years. The final year of that Lee wasn't playing with us – with anyone – and I was, and that was hard. Actually, it was always hard,' she laughed. 'There was nothing easy about him.'

It wasn't a snide laugh, not the sort you might imagine after all that happened. In this light it didn't look too bad, not as bad as he'd described it. From the tip of her eye, down her cheek, to her mouth; I made a mental note to notice it outside.

Such a strong picture I'd had of her, it didn't match up. Maybe it was the way she'd dressed for court; or the years that had passed in the meantime. Lee's first girlfriend, Lee's only girlfriend, the girl he talked so much about. The things I know about Lizzie.

She said, 'Our relationship was tempestuous, we sparked each other off. Maybe it was our age, or the whole situation, maybe it was him – I've never been like that with anyone else. But I'd never met anyone like him.

'He was always having to prove himself. He was the youngest in the orchestra, he was Michael's protégé, he wasn't good enough, really, to justify his position. But he made up for that with his energy, he put everything into his music.

'He had to, I guess. He lived with Michael, he didn't have any escape.

'He was so enthusiastic, though, so alive, I liked that. He could be touchy, moody, he'd take things to heart, the least little incident would make him go off, but I liked that too. We were always falling out, falling in love, I'd never had that passion. I had this crazy notion it added to my playing.

'But everything was intense for him like it wasn't for me. The orchestra was his life and his prison depending on his mood. The other members were his family one minute, but he couldn't trust them the next . . . James was an antidote to all of us.

'Lee used to go off and hang out with James, it was breathing space, it was a different life. He didn't do it that much at first, but more often as the years went on, and for longer. It was the only time when I didn't have him, it was the only thing that kept him from me. In that respect, I suppose, James was the enemy. James was my rival.

'But it was down to him that we were never in the same camp. Because even if they were just having a drink on a Friday night I wasn't welcome, James didn't want me along. He'd try to make trouble between us, he'd pull his cousin Lara out of the bag – Lee had a thing about Lara. He'd give Lee coke and get him manic so for two days afterwards he'd be moody and aggressive. He could be a spoilt brat. He'd say things we wouldn't dare to say to Michael, like an adolescent with his dad. He'd cause scenes and have tantrums to get what he wanted. Not often. But always after he'd spent time with James.

'I couldn't see what Lee saw in him. They were opposite ends of the spectrum. Lee was warm, generous; James cold, awkward and mean. When James graduated he played jingles for adverts; Lee lived for his music. That sums up the difference between them.

'And that was one of the ways James got to him. He'd say things like, "You don't get enough exposure" or "I see Cabresi's given so-and-so the Elgar" or, "He's not the only conductor in the world".

'James unsettled him. He put him off his stride, off his work, with his little comments, with his nights on the town. He went out of his way to mess up Lee's life, I fought that. Perhaps the battle was all in my head. Perhaps James was just being himself without any tactics. But he won in the end, that's how I saw it.

'He became our one argument, the final row that all our rows led up to. In some way I was jealous – he held an attraction. And I couldn't understand that attraction.

'We broke up when I found out about Lara, we'd been together six years, that was down to James. He rang me once asking for Lee, Lee had said he'd be with James, he was with Lara, I'm sure James did it on purpose, I'm sure he knew all about it, it was awful. An awful time. Lee was unbearable once we split up, on some sort of mission to be as unpleasant as possible. He was rude, he got this idea in his head that we were holding him back, that he was destined for stardom. He accused Michael of favouritism towards other players. Things came to a head and he left.

'But he couldn't just leave the orchestra, he also had to leave Michael, he had to find somewhere else to live. He moved in with James.

'Then, everything was over. We got back together, we dragged it out for quite a long time but really it was over, everything was finished, everything changed.

'There was no reason at all why he shouldn't have got another job except for the road he went down with James. They were out every night, partying, clubbing, Lee liked that lifestyle – and then he was especially susceptible. James had nothing to get up for.

'I didn't notice at the time how all of it affected Lee, leaving the orchestra, leaving his home (he'd lived with Michael for ten years by the time he moved out). I just saw the constant drug taking, drinking, just saw Lee on a permanent bender. He was working here and there, playing at weddings, that kind of thing, but he couldn't get work in an orchestra. It was a vicious circle, he realized that, but he wouldn't do anything about it.

'He became a different person, manic, on edge, he was busy all the time doing nothing. He had so much energy it scared me but he never got anything done. He couldn't sit still, couldn't sleep, he stopped eating. I didn't want to watch it any more when there was nothing I could do.

'He had an audition coming up that he was pinning his hopes on. I knew he wouldn't get through. I was so involved, I was so desperate, I thought giving it up would be a relief. He screamed at me, "Pick your moment!" when I told him, but it wasn't like that. My heart was broken.

'And it wasn't a relief either, it was worse when I wasn't there to keep an eye on him. I was going crazy thinking about him, worrying about him, what was he up to, what was James up to without me there to rein things in. A few days later I bumped into James. He was going out that night with Lee. I asked him where. I just wanted to speak to him. I just wanted to make sure he was okay. I waited. I had a bit too much to drink. Lee came in with James and Lara. He was completely off his head. I thought, You're not friends to him, and I went for her. He rushed to her defence.'

Fifty-one

How history repeats itself. Five years later a similar scene would be playing again. Lee, high as you like, performing for Lara; Gina looking on in horror and disbelief. That night, herald of a major decline, just as this night is. This night ending a career; that night – everything.

And even though she's with James now Gina couldn't help but implicate him. 'It was the beginning of the end,' she said, 'the beginning of their terrible row.' Bitter, malicious, foul play and dirty tricks. And then, the dirtiest trick of all.

Fifty-two

I was in the club that night with a boy I had met a few weeks before. We were having a drink at the bar when Lee rushed in. He went for James. Grabbed him, shouted right in his face, 'You've gone too far this time! You're over.' Two days later he was dead. If James didn't kill him, who else did?

Fifty-three

Mrs Barker walks her dog at nine o'clock. He's not as young as he used to be, she isn't either, this stroll around the block was once a quick stretch before bed, it now takes half an hour. She's sure of that. She does it each evening. On September 6th she came back through the gate of her front garden and saw James coming out of the house next door. She's sure of that too. Very definitely coming out. Well, at least, not knocking, or ringing the doorbell, not going in, not trying to. She knows Lee. He takes Oscar for walks in the park sometimes when she isn't able to. She's met James. On that evening he was out of sorts, he seemed cross when she said hello to him, he was gruff, almost rude. 'He was obviously annoyed that I'd spotted him.'

'Could it not be, Mrs Barker,' posed the Defence, 'that the Defendant, rather than being annoyed because you'd "spotted" him, as you put it, was actually annoyed because he'd been invited to Lee's house, but having made the journey, found nobody there to answer the door?'

'I don't know about that.'

'Do you think that it's possible?'

'I don't know.'

'Yes, you don't know whether it's true. Do you think that it's possible?'

'I suppose so.'

'Thank you, Mrs Barker. Nothing further.'

'Mrs Barker,' said the Prosecution, 'as far as you know, did anyone else come in or out of Lee's house that evening?'

'No.'

'Thank you. No further questions.'

Fifty-four

Three dreaded words, each person ticked off, each narrative ended, another step closer to the verdict. I've longed for it and I've feared it and now it's tomorrow. While this trial continues my head is still full of his life ... Bit by bit I'll cease to remember – the exact shape of his mouth when he made that remark, the day that he made it, what happened next – I'll forget. But the paradox of the broken heart is the pain at the thought of its going away.

The end of the day. We rise. James is led away. Days, at least, have an external chatter, albeit macabre, the evenings are far worse. Then the chatter is all in my head. There, episodes flash out in no reasonable order. In the quiet of my flat, in my solitude, I see his face, I see his face, I see his face.

PART TWO

One

I am familiar with this journey now, a regular along the bus route. Often I see the same old faces and I wonder if they register mine. How do their days compare? When I was a child and I'd done something wrong I'd get this same feeling seeing other people. Other people on the street or on the bus or in my home who didn't know the thing I'd done, who didn't know what was going to happen to me once I got caught, for whom this whole massive incident wouldn't mean a thing. How big could it be, then? How bad? It didn't work, it doesn't now. I try to imagine the woman across the aisle or the man standing up, holding the strap above me, imagine their absence of my grief, their utter ignorance of my feeling, for a second it's comforting, but I'm me again.

The streets tell me I'm me as I walk again along them, we recognize each other, this parking meter and I, I'm part of this landscape, this morning's shop windows show me my reflection, this key fits into this front door, this lift, the 7th floor, the coat where I left it, the half-drunk coffee on the table, the objects I scatter round me, the view—

The view that never fails to stop my breath.

Rumbling, buzzing, living, dying, carrying on beneath me. Cacophony of individual moments melded, the bigger picture. Tiny fractions of teardrops that make up a wave that makes up the ocean. Where am I in this? Safe inside my windows that look onto a city that doesn't know I'm here.

Two

Watching, feeling invisible, it seems I always come back to these windows. The first time I looked out of them, the city at my fingertips, feeling I didn't belong, not yet; feeling my heart beat when I caught the lift downstairs, stepped out into it, got swept along by its current I didn't care where. Places, people, faces, clothes all fascinated me, the rush, the noise, the vibe of the city, feeling I was in its midst for a while but it was just an illusion, I came out the other side. Back to this side, hands pressed up against the windows; watching, feeling invisible.

Three

I had friends once, I had lots of friends, I was known in places like the Orange Room. I went to clubs and danced all night, out for dinner, out for lunch, out for a quick drink before a party somewhere else, I had friends once, I had lots of friends.

But it wasn't possible to keep living like that, looking for meaning in interaction, looking for security there, something real and lasting. I used friends as ballast, something to hold me down. I thought I would know who I was in relation. My place in the scheme of things. This is my life.

I used to tell them – I feel, I don't feel, why?, what do you think? Too much information, then. No one road to walk down. If I pick this apple I won't have picked that other one. If I behave like this, like, how shall I behave? What do you think, you think, you think? Really? Who do you think I am? Am I? What do I think? I don't know, I forget.

I came in. Once in, out seemed so ridiculous.

A different apartness to the one I feel now. A sort of zen I'd reached, a calm. It's easy not to be lonely when there isn't someone in particular you miss, some need unmet. I didn't have need. I had no vested interest in the way that events turned out, no personal involvement, no room for disappointment, I had grown another skin. I had perfected the art of being alone.

Four

'I don't have any skin,' he says to me, the first time he meets me. He sits on the swivel chair opposite, staring at his knees. The last two fingers on his left hand bend and jut out, the result of a fight he's been in, I have it in my notes. 'I don't have any skin,' he says to me, 'that's what it feels like. Everything hurts.'

He doesn't say much, well it's hard the first time, disconcerting; speaking seemingly into a void, words directed at a person trained not to respond.

I study him. Long body crunched up, crouched into the back of that swivel chair, he'd tuck himself up in it if he could. Layers of clothes despite the heat, replacing his lost skin, presumably. Hair stuck flat against his forehead, hands visibly trembling, jaw trembling, speech slow. 'I don't know what this is,' he says eventually, 'it's like brain flu.'

Five

Unimportant at the time, although, on some level it can't have been. I remember it. I remember it all. I remember the bits of it I never knew. Perhaps it's not his story after all, but mine.

Meeting Lee was remembering summer in the middle of winter. Wrapped up, dodging the rain, scarf wound tight against the cold, a sudden break in the wind, the sun reflected off the white wall of a building by which you're standing, a fraction of brightness, a moment of heat . . .

Why? Why him? Why now? This man is broken but I'm used to broken people. At first he's like the rest, someone to whom I listen who elicits no response, whose journey's very different to my own, who reinforces my smug calm, but then, but then . . .

Six

The fight remains unmentioned although I know that's why he's here. Instead he lists his symptoms: he's become very sensitive to light and sound; if he wants to watch telly he has to turn the brightness down; he can hardly bear the noisy voices on his answerphone; he's afraid to go outside . . . Fear envelops him. Even standing close to the window makes his heart start to race until it's all he can do to lie down and breathe . . .

Lying in bed, thinking of showering, it terrifies him. He goes through each step one by one. First sit up, put feet on the floor, put one foot in front of the other down the corridor, reach the bathroom, turn on the taps – he tries it but he panics. Sweat, tears, a thumping in his head, he lies down again. Do I know what it cost him to get here? It took him two hours. Once, it would have taken a third of that.

'What's happening to me?' he asks slowly. 'What is this?'

What should I say? Clinical depression? Nervous breakdown? Exhaustion? Nothing so unspecific would satisfy him. He'd want a map: the illness works like this, this is exactly what's malfunctioning. What should I say? Nobody knows.

He has started to calcify. There's a thread from his knees to his shoulders that by steady degrees is being pulled taut. There's no air in him, no room, he can't pull himself free from himself, he has to tell himself to breathe. Inside, moving from one room to another, he doesn't notice how slowly he walks, but outside, he can't cross the road before the green man goes red. He wants to lie under a shelf, hide in a cupboard. He doesn't fit. Instead he ties his clothes round his shoulders and makes himself inside his bed. 'I switch on the telly,' he says, 'and I'm thinking, please keep telling me things, please keep up your noise and drown out the noise in my head.' And I remember imagining, as I hadn't with anyone else, the life of this creature after he'd left my office. His journey home. The ordeal of the bus. Strangers. Getting on and getting off. Crossing the road. Walking. All these things which not long ago had been unnoticeable, now terrify. That peculiar shift of reality. Unbelievable, inexplicable. *Why? What's happening to me?*

The mind keeps its secrets.

Seven

We are not our own masters. What was it about him? Was it all in my head? In the quiet of my flat I listen. Sounds that were once a comfort for me. This home, like a body, gurgles and creaks, performs its own upkeep invisibly. Water fills pipes as they empty, electricity stores in the walls ready for action. This place once fed me, kept me warm, protected me from out there. Just a noise, the world beyond, just a hum. Then I brought it in with me.

Eight

He wept. He wouldn't stop weeping. He found it hideous, embarrassing, he likened it to being sick, saying to your body, Please, no more, I can't stand it, your body responding by throwing up.

'I can't do anything,' he tells me, 'anything at all. Everything is too much. Today I went to the fridge to get out some milk and I couldn't reach it. *That* made me cry. That!' he says, as though his mind is at odds with itself.

But it is.

There are things that he knows. He knows he's got skin, he knows he won't spill if he doesn't tie clothes round his shoulders, he knows nothing will happen to him on the way to the bathroom. But there is something else directing him. Some overwhelming thing.

'Like having a bad trip,' he says, 'but not like I'm completely wasted. Part of me is sober. I'm not just tripping, I'm going "Oh my God I'm tripping", which is worse.'

*   *   *

'My bad trip gets worse,' he tells me, 'because bits of it are real. People are out to get me, even if it's only pushing me out of their way because I'm walking so slowly. People stare at me. Because I look like . . . a freak. I don't want them to see me, shuffling along, unshaven and dirty. I try to make myself smaller. Scrunch myself up till I ache.'

'And then, occasionally, I am completely fine. A couple of hours a day.'

'Respite?'

'Yes.' He looks up for a moment and I'm struck by something in his eyes. Something I like. Something that frightens me.

Nine

Before I met Lee I knew what to do with my evenings. Eat. Make eating a ritual. A treat. Put on some music. A glass of red wine. Bury myself in my work. Look up, occasionally, out at the view. Stand up. Walk to the window. It interests me but it doesn't quite touch me. I find something like comfort in that.

What to do now, though? No hunger in me. No armour against the terrible sadness of music, no room in my head for work, no room for anything else. Red wine. A glass of red wine and the view. I can lose myself for a moment or two . . .

Ten

... It's not just his fingers that are broken, so is he, his sense of self, the future he'd imagined. Who could he be if he couldn't be a cellist? Still he doesn't tell me how it happened. I wait for him. I know. And finally they start to come out, the details of that evening.

It was hazy, buying them both a drink; turning round to see Liz with a broken bottle in her hand, catching it in his before it got to Lara, the pain and the reflex action, it was just a reflex action—

He didn't see them again until it went to court. He tried to phone Lara but she wouldn't take his calls. Nobody would. He left messages for Cabresi. He tried to explain to Bob. But Bob saw things in black and white and Lee had broken some fundamental code. The one who upset him the most, though, was Lara. It had all been for her. If he hadn't intervened her face would have been slashed, instead of which his fingers were. The last two fingers on his left hand. The most important ones.

Strangely enough, he held it together until after the verdict. He was fine when it happened, the drama of it, the cut to his hand, the waiting to see if he'd be able to play, finding he couldn't, he didn't go to pieces then, not till after the verdict, not till after 'not guilty'. That's when he went into shock. That's when his body stopped functioning.

He'd been lucky not to go to jail, he knows that, but somehow this just makes things worse. His lawyer pleaded provocation and defence, he'd come to the aid of another, who knows what might have happened if he hadn't? But he felt like a fraud when he was let off the hook. He must have done something wrong or Lara would still be speaking to him, his parents would not be ashamed of him, his friends would not be ignoring him; and if he hadn't done anything wrong then his career is over and it isn't his fault, his whole life is over and he hasn't deserved it. It's too much for his mind to compute, it's an information overload. How should I feel? How should I react? How much is my responsibility? How much should I resent? It's easier to lie under his duvet letting it hold him, comforting, consoling, wanting nothing back. He sleeps more than he's awake, huge, heavy sleeps that he has to claw his way out of, imagining there is something on the other side demanding his attention, then, when he is conscious and realizes there's nothing, he falls asleep again.

Eleven

Is it fear of life or fear of death? I have read that in this country, twenty people die each year getting out of bed. Twenty are electrocuted by alarm clocks, thirty drowned in baths, sixty seriously hurt just putting on their socks, six hundred killed falling down the stairs ... Life is risk. Is depression fear of life or fear of death?

He has no appetite. He has no sex-drive. These acts – eating, reproducing – ensure one's survival. If depression has evolved, if it has a reason, is it to keep its victims alive or to kill them? ... Because life is all about species culling themselves.

Twelve

I have more of an in-road than most into intimate moments. I'm the fly on the wall, the imaginary friend. He tells me all, as though I'm never really there, not judging (isn't that the point?), not making any judgment. He doesn't give reasons, simply presents the facts. He'd been drunk. He'd done a lot of coke. Lizzie had swung for Lara with a broken glass which he had intercepted. He'd been clumsier than he would have been sober, it was tragic – for him and for her – it was an accident.

But it wasn't really an accident. It might have been if he'd left it at that. Why are you so angry? I wonder, What is it? Where's the source? Why are you so angry? I remember wondering. Not just because of the evening described in my notes and then from his lips, but because of the look in his eye, that occasional glint, his old self. Something passionate but also furious, something utterly beguiling, joyful but cruel, intriguing and frightening. A childish look.

Thirteen

This time of the day could be morning or evening, just about to get light, just about to get dark, the sky smudgy and dull. I don't turn on the lamps, I don't flick any switches, I want to be able to watch with no light in the window, I want to remain invisible. There's relief that the world carries on, indifferent to me, doesn't notice whether I'm here or I'm not; whether Lee is; all of this unnecessary.

I could blot myself out in the night, in this flat. But my

mind won't stop telling his story. Like some curse. Like some sort of punishment. Comforting and terrible, the hours and hours of dark before me.

Fourteen

He always called it 'the accident' but it wasn't really, it might have been if he'd left it at that. He was found not guilty, but nevertheless he had to see me – his temper must be attended to. And anyway, once off the hook his mind imposed its own reproof, its own prison sentence, so his sessions with me were fortunate. That strange vortex he found himself in, his struggle to adapt, the battle against the way he was behaving, sanity versus delirium.

Once his shock wore off, misery set in. He talked, tears flowing down his cheeks, almost unaware of them. Weeping was a given. He told me all the awful things he'd done: the way he'd hurt his parents; the pain he'd caused, ignorant at the time; the things he took for granted: love, Cabresi's generosity; the chances he'd been given, thrown away; the way he'd treated others, thought of them, pitched lower down some imagined scale of evolution. He felt he deserved what he'd got. Not because of what happened with Lizzie and Lara, not because of that evening, but his whole life to date. He'd had no regard, no respect. His lack of consideration, his arrogance, they were enough to bring him down. He couldn't play, he could barely live, well, he'd had it coming. He was sure of that. That evening with Lara and Lizzie, there was so much coincidence involved. He was certain it was destined in some way.

But nothing further could happen now that could hurt him. He had jumped out of the world everyone else was inhabiting and had moved into some other realm. The dead undead. There was nothing that could touch him here. There was nothing that could make things worse. There was no one who could knock him off his perch, because, he had no perch to sit on.

He'd taken a cab to the session. The radio was on in the front. He could hear a song that was big last summer and remembered dancing to it. Dancing to it in nightclubs, at parties, flirting with girls, grinning all over his face, getting high, getting trashed, going home with someone, being happy. Another world. Another life. He couldn't imagine enjoying those things ever again and this made him worry. He was frightened there was no way out of this spiral. Nothing to recover to. These days, there was so much adrenaline in him, his pupils were constantly dilated. The bright lights of Tesco's were too bright. They made him panic.

'There's no way this will go away,' he said, 'because what happened can't unhappen.'

Fifteen

Poor, mad creature. Poor precarious boy.

It's when you start talking you realize your essential aloneness; you have to explain. In this way I undo what I set out to heal. There's no love between patient and therapist, no solidarity, we're not in the same boat you and I, I'm fine, and you're not. You explain yourself to me in more detail than usual and I'll show you how different I am, how alone you are.

But how alone I am too. Suddenly this space I've made seems ridiculous, isolated. Describing your apartness makes me see mine, makes the way I've been living a form of madness, both of us locked within our heads; both of us the same.

Sixteen

Now he starts to mention someone called James. James comes and sits with him, James is the only one who's safe. James owns the flat they live in, James was there the night it happened, James got him his lawyer – everything was paid for by his good friend James.

James seems to know how to deal with him, leave him alone, take no notice of his curious behaviour. His lack of skin, it means that everything hurts, everything gets in: love, concern – reaction. James barely registers he's there. James makes no comment; 'Ignores me; like you do.'

James stopped charging rent when his money ran out. He doesn't know what would have happened if he hadn't had James. James is the only one who's stuck by him. The only person he's got in the world is James; 'and you, you don't count, though.'

He'd been going to be the best. He had to be. To spite his parents, to excuse his arrogance, to explain his outlandish behaviour. Now, he'll be nothing. He's developed a fear of all those he's been rude to, sneered at, blanked, the ones who'd been waiting to watch him fall. He imagines them out there, out to get him. He wraps his duvet even more tightly around him and thinks, in here I am safe. He's grateful he doesn't have to be here alone.

James doesn't fuss him, doesn't make him eat or wake up or help in any way but carries on as normal. He's a pet, some peculiar dependant from whom nothing is expected but his presence. It's all he wants to be.

James just lets him sit there. James lets him sit there. James just sits there, demanding nothing, offering nothing, watching TV. And when he does go out again, eventually, James is always with him.

Seventeen

If I were James how would I be? When I can barely resist responding to you, would I be a help or a hindrance, would I be 'safe' if I were in James's position, free to act? What would I do?

James doesn't do anything wrong, but doesn't he bleed? Is he made of stone? Not to react in the least little way to your shocking behaviour, your (I presume) enormous demise. Who is this man? Where has he sprung from? Is he just careless, or cruel? Awakened or indifferent? Part of me can't help but admire such apathy; such supreme detachment is something I flattered myself I had mastered. But you, your warmth, your power, the feeling behind your broken front . . .

'He doesn't understand,' you say, as if you know what I'm thinking, 'He's perfect to be with but he doesn't know what it's like. He said, "You're lucky because you're really, really alive," but no, I am really dead. The world is carrying on without me.'

Eighteen

But after a while he figured out how to handle it. He'd set himself one thing to do per day. Some days he'd be able to do this thing – take a bath, go to the corner shop – others he'd feel fine until he had to do it, then he'd find himself in tears. On these days he'd give up and make himself a cup of tea. He'd treat himself to a bit of daytime TV. He'd watch *Classic Homes* in bed perhaps. Perhaps he'd take a Valium. And after he figured out how to handle it, it changed.

Things do change, but imperceptibly, it's a tease. You can't get a purchase on the process. All the time imagining life stays the same, fending off a vague depression at the inevitable sameness of days, waking up in the morning with a sick ache in your gut which you can't quite attribute, but which may be the fear that today's going to be just like yesterday, finding some comfort in that, but things change, imperceptibly.

Nineteen

I started buying cello music. In the evenings I'd go home and listen to it. The day would end as it's ending now, the colour of the sky this colour, shade after subtle shade duller, unnoticeable – then dark suddenly. The city an oddly appropriate backdrop to the music, funny sometimes,

sometimes faintly tragic. This car replacing that car in a steady stream of traffic lights, like notes, the humdrum of the evening: leaving here, coming back, passing in-between, plans made on mobile phones, buses caught, roads crossed, all above this baleful music, almost breathed, sighed out.

If I could go backwards, if it could be then, could I stem the tide, could I turn the course of events? In retrospect all I see is cause and effect, it was all I felt at the time. No way to undo what's already done, to cancel a cause long forgotten. I am Lee, this is what I do, no way to restitch that pattern.

And then he was angry. Angry that his career was over. Angry that because of two stupid girls ... He should have let them have it, should have let them get on with it – both of them had tried to manipulate him. And if he'd left them alone, if Lara had been hurt and Liz had gone to jail then no one would have thought he'd done anything wrong. His fucking dad, who went on about being gentlemanly and behaving like a man, wouldn't have thought he'd done anything wrong. The whole world was fucked. His dad who never supported him anyway. His mum who always agreed with his dad. They'd thought he was bad, he was difficult, well now they were right, now he was. He'd never wanted to be anything different. He'd never wanted to be anything special. Fucking cello. He would have been a normal guy. Fucking Michael Cabresi who put ideas in his head. He told him he was talented and then he held him back. The faggot probably just fancied him. Fucking everyone wanted something from him. Well, fuck you all! Fuck you! and fuck you!

Twenty

But things were turning. He was starting to get better bit by bit, his anger being the herald of this. He would suddenly notice – he'd made a phone call, laughed at something on the radio, caught himself whistling walking down the street. Walking! Not shuffling. His tremors stopped, normal sleep returned, his body relaxed, tongue loosened up.

He didn't push himself. Nothing too taxing. He didn't go out socializing, nothing like that. The thought of that would send him into a tailspin, heart rushing, head dizzy, panic attack. But he could go to the supermarket, he could go to the greasy caff, he could even go for a drink – if it was to any old pub. Nothing special. Nowhere trendy, he couldn't have that. But surely, it was only a matter of time . . .

I watched his struggle with a mix of optimism and despair. *You'll get there*, tempered with an uneasy foreboding, clairvoyance of the next time he'd go to pieces.

Was it self-fulfilling prophecy?

I'd listen to Tchaikovsky's Concerto No. 4 . . . Schumann's in A . . . Elgar's in E – quite exquisitely beautiful then, when life was painless, quite unacceptable now that it's not.

I draw the curtains.

Twenty-one

I switch on the lights. See how warm it is, how snug, the world shut out now, cosy in here. My turning inward was simultaneous with a need to redecorate, to buffer my fortress, stock the bunker, everything chosen to please the eye, calm the spirit, comfort the body from the stress of outside. But one step, another, there is always more, it became something bigger than simply not engaging, it was altogether opting out, a celibacy of body and mind. As though desire was not of my making but something imposed. As though nature was ridiculous, careless of me, forcing my hand, roping me into this unending cycle of birth and death. Not any more.

It was similar for Lee.

Similar, but not the same. I could spend my life in my head; he was a very physical person. Tactile. His retreat showed up in his body, his body that now was gaining strength again. I willed him to recovery. He was my hope. If he could do it, so could I. So must I. My duty.

Twenty-two

I started buying cello music. In the evenings I'd go home and listen to it, over and over, until I'd mapped it in my head, then I'd replace it with a newer purchase. I started buying listings magazines. I don't remember when this began, or what whetted my appetite. Lee's speech had long been peppered with musical references, pieces he'd played, composers he admired, cellists he'd once wished to emulate. It wasn't this information so much as his casual mention of venues, rehearsal spaces, backstage attitudes and behaviour, the absolutely alien portrayed to me as though I too found it familiar. I started buying listings magazines and flipping to their music section. This gave a voyeuristic tingle of pleasure soon to be replaced by a proprietorial one. I knew that concerto, Lee had talked of that conductor, his favourite place to play was once that concert hall.

It wasn't long before I started going. Not just imagining the arrangement of the musicians, the looks on their faces, the meditative quality of the audience, but experiencing it. I'd supposed this reality would be a bit of a disappointment. I'd been to concerts on a few occasions but never without constantly checking the programme, without feeling let down if I'd estimated we were further on than we actually were. I thought I wouldn't enjoy myself as much as I had in my head, in my living room, adjusting the volume on the cd, wandering into the kitchen, swinging my arms in the hall. But I'd a vested interest now. It belonged to me, this world. I knew things about it that I bet that man on my right didn't know, that woman there with her eyes closed, the couple who left in the interval. If there was a cellist I'd imagine him as Lee. I tried not to miss the concerts Cabresi conducted.

Something so terribly sweet and so tragic. All of this gone. This friendship with Cabresi. This community. This way of life. He's angry, he's self-pitying, I understand that; but not his optimism, his getting back on his feet. His excitement that he's moving. That James has bought a hovel of a house. That he's going to employ him to do it up; let him live there. A place of his own. A project. A job.

From musician to builder in under two years.

Twenty-three

I had this uneasy foreboding. A sense from the moment he began to get well, that sooner or later he'd break down again. I'd tell myself, When the brain goes into overload it always bears the scars, and scar tissue's delicate, weak, more likely to be injured again. I'd say, Thought processes are maps which the brain remembers. Of course it might happen again – it's easier to follow old routes than to make up new ones. But this was like prophecy. Then, was it self-fulfilling? Was it my fault, then? 'I've started over once,' he'd say to me, 'I don't think I can do it again.'

I'd agree.

If only I hadn't agreed.

I've been over it, though. I've been over it so many times. I tell myself: I had my reasons. I made my choice.

Twenty-four

James sets off warning bells the moment he enters Lee's story, eight months after we meet, ten months before he gets well. Nothing logical, it's instinctive, I dismiss it as I'm trained to. I've no idea what he looks like, I invent him a face, white skin, cruel mouth, weak eyes, for no palpable reason. He looks after Lee – feeds him, houses him – but there's something that feels not quite right, not quite healthy. I read between the lines of the stories Lee tells me. College days, James's enduring friendship, I see them, it hurts to see them, why does it hurt to see them?

Because James takes advantage of a vulnerable boy. Because James makes Lee his own. Because, how much of what happened was planned by him? Encouraging Lee to doubt Cabresi so then he'd leave the orchestra; pumping him up with drink and drugs so then he'd split with Lizzie; so then that night with Lara—

And now he's bought a place to house his creature.

He's rich and his money makes money. He's the sort of person who always gets a lucky break. For a while he was playing jingles for adverts, messing about, then someone he worked with pointed out his beautiful voice, suggested he should get into selling advertising space. He was fantastically successful. While Lee lay in bed James made fat commissions on top of his salary. It was easy money. Behind a telephone he could charm, beguile, tease and persuade. He already had the capital to set up a business, he took his best colleagues with him, he was made. He barely had to go to work if he didn't want to.

He bought a little house round the corner from his flat. A dilapidated terraced house that Lee could live in. Lee could do it up. He'd be doing him a favour, really, giving him some cash and a bit of responsibility. Certainly, Lee saw it like that. Maybe that's how it was.

The house was in a dreadful state. The previous owner had been elderly, had lived there all his married life, had died there. His clothes were still in the cupboards, his pictures still hung on the walls. It was a sad house, dark, damp, cold, there was no central heating.

It hurts me to recall Lee's optimism. The spirit in his voice when he'd describe his plans, discussions with the architect, his opinion taken seriously. It would take two years, he reckoned, getting it right. Walls knocked down, rooms built, new kitchen, new bathroom, loft conversion, extension at the back. He described his vision in detail. I knew that house by heart.

Downstairs were four poky rooms, three leading into each other. The one on its own was the first that you came to, to the right of the front door. Down the hall was a little – Lee didn't know how to describe it, he thought 'room' too generous a word for it. A sort of cordoned-off section of the corridor. A window looking onto a brick wall opposite a decrepit gas fire, on either side of which, two depressed-looking chairs. The carpet was curling, wallpaper bubbled and went green, the window panes were rotten. There was a sliding glass door in the third wall, corrugated so you couldn't see through it, which led into the kitchen. A cooker, a fridge, a cupboard. No washing machine – no room. The floor was covered with red linoleum tiles and bits of food, and cans of peaches and salmon and carrots were stacked by the door to the bathroom. This had obviously been added on, the door into it from the kitchen was once the back door. Outside the grass was knee-high. There weren't any flowerbeds. It came to an end by a wooden fence over which some sort of creeper was growing abundantly. The space was large, large enough to build an extension and still have room for a decent garden.

Upstairs were three little bedrooms. Two looked onto the garden, one looked onto the street. Lee decided to sleep in the latter, the best of a bad bunch, obviously the old man's room; there was a gas fire in there, at least.

It was winter, and as a temporary measure he sealed up the windows with polythene to stop the draughts and the leaks. He would have ripped up the musty carpet and washed the floor but it was cold, he'd need to put rugs down, he couldn't afford them; he would have chucked out the mattress on the old man's bed and got a new one, but he had no cash. It smelled foetid in there, damp warmed up a little, grandpa's smell.

To me it seemed like cruelty, making him live there, showing who's boss. And when he started working, the barbs James threw at him. He didn't seem to notice. I did, but I'd think I was transferring so tiny were the comments, so small, the way Lee told them so innocuous: '"Isn't it weird the way that things work out?" James said the other day, "You, working for me, who would have thought it?"'

'He loved the cupboard. He said, "It's amazing. Six months ago you couldn't make a cup of tea."

'"You've got a real talent for this. Perhaps you've found your vocation."'

One day the world was his, his whole life before him, the places he'd go, the things that he'd do; the next he would cling to James's little house, 'thank God because what else could I do? I can't play music. I've got no real education. I could teach I suppose.' I could just hear James say it.

But Lee never noticed.

All the time thinking, 'Wish I could tell you . . .' Mentally, trying to undo their friendship. Stopping at all the points I have mapped where it might have failed but stayed strong. After his breakdown, when he met Lizzie, once he left college, meeting in the first place . . . If only it hadn't been

James. Fate seems to throw them together, then keep them there. But in the back of my mind, persistently, nagging, is the thought that something else binds them. Something intrinsic to Lee that chooses the friendship of someone like James.

Twenty-five

I must eat. I haven't eaten all day. Food, the buying of it, the preparation, the pulling it out of the oven or off the stove as a present to myself, was such an integral part of my evening, one of the landmarks which broke up the hours: supper, then a bit of work, bath, a programme on the radio, bed. Now I don't have tastebuds. I eat because my body demands it, it doesn't matter what – ready-meals I used to be smug about, beans on toast, cheesy-egg – I stuff them down as though I'm starving, as though my mind hasn't noticed but my body has, as though it can't rely on me to feed it again.

He was such a physical being. Long, pulled up and proud. His presence, like a technicolour aura, made him more than three-dimensional, almost superimposed. He was wonderful to look at. The flint in his eyes, the crease in his chin, that waist extended like a dancer's, the length of his limbs. And him, him inside his body, his warmth, his wanting to know, himself first, others after, his interest, his instinct to touch, tactile as a child.

But rage could fill him, drink could, drugs. Working on that house of James's, it was an accident waiting to happen, a bomb on a slow-burning fuse. James was rich and on the make, Lee proud, talented and ruined. They were friends once, now they're master and servant, it couldn't help but explode.

Overlying all of this, the gratitude Lee owes him. He's grateful, of course he is, he tells me all the time, he can't believe what James has done: stuck by him, paid his way, given him a home, a job – but in that position you can't be quite grateful enough. Favours like that never work. If you pick someone up when they're down and expect nothing back, perhaps, but more often you want something back; there's always that politic: I've saved you, but for me . . . Wouldn't it make you feel stronger next to someone wretched like that? Wouldn't it make you feel powerful? Necessary? Kind? Then when they need you no longer—

James binds Lee to him, the tricks he pulls to keep him.

Twenty-six

'The first time I took cocaine,' he says to me, 'was about a month after I met Lizzie. James bought it. Well, he could afford to. It was a Friday afternoon and we were going out later. We always go out on a Friday night, it's like our ritual . . . I stayed in for over two years after what happened, but six months ago, when I began to get well, we started again. The only place I can go, though, is the pub round the corner. I've this crazy aversion to all our old haunts, all those self-conscious places we used to hang out in. James wants to go back, or else somewhere new, more exciting. I don't know though, I can't for some reason.

'He said, "Go on, you'll be fine, you'll love it," but I

couldn't be persuaded. Some sort of fear I've got. I want to get past it because it's really important not to be scared, to get back into being sociable again, being young. I'm twenty-nine now. I've lost three years. My twenties have nearly run out.

'He said, "Go on, do a line of coke," but I couldn't. I got into a panic about my medication having some reaction to it. He laughed at me. He said, "You've really changed. My God!" He said, "All right, but I'm going out with Tim then. I can't stand another evening in that pub." Tim's some guy he works with—'

Suddenly I see the whole thing sliding away. I think, This man is bad for Lee. I think, If only I could say . . .

But what could I say? What could I do? Even if he wasn't my patient what difference could I make, a middle-aged man?

Mentally, though, I wage war with James. Think of strategies for beating him; ways of becoming an influence without expressing an opinion. I come up with nothing. I despair, gain hope, bide my time. Something opportune must happen, someone fitting come along—

Twenty-seven

One day he says to me, 'I went out in town last night. I loved it, I absolutely fucking loved it. God, I can't believe I've stayed in all this time,' there's a twinkle in his eye, 'I didn't even want to go,' he says, 'I was just doing it for James. There's some girl he's into, she was going to some bar . . . I had such a good time. Felt a bit paranoid at one

point but James got in a round, then cut me a line in the
toilet. Just one. Just because I felt a bit weird. You don't
approve, do you?' A pause. 'Do you?'

'You should just be aware,' I say, 'cocaine brings on the
superman condition.'

'Hmm?'

'The sense that you are unstoppable.'

'Well I *was* unstoppable that night. I scored. Can you
believe it? I hadn't had sex for nearly three years, not since
this,' he holds up his fingers. 'Look at me! I'm young, in
my prime, I'm good looking. It's been such a waste, all
this time.'

Well, he made up for it now. He was not going to love,
never again, look where it got him, Lizzie had broken his
heart, Lara had abandoned him. This was what he needed.
This was perfect. The type of girls he slept with were the
kind who woke up in the morning and said 'See you', the
grown-up kind. It wasn't just Fridays he went out with
James, it was any time he felt like, it was three nights a
week. He didn't have to get up early for work. Neither did
James. They went out on the town. They took every drug
they could lay their hands on.

Twenty-eight

I suddenly feel like a bath. I want to immerse myself in
steaming, hot water. Let out my breath, sink down to the
bottom, breathe in again, float to the top; imagine the
water flowing into every orifice, filling them up, swilling
them out. I run one. The things that he did to his body,

that extraordinary body, the girls he let touch it.

I was Lee once. Not so priapic, I never had his beauty. But I used to go out all the time. I'd feel important in the right places, with the right people, I had friends once, I had lots of friends.

I came in, though, it was a struggle, I had to feel it was right. I had to disregard all those who continued to behave as I had, leading the life I had wanted for so many years but could never quite grasp, never quite hold in my hand. I was aware of these feelings when I listened to Lee, tried to discount my negativity as personal prejudice.

But he did start to change. Started to revert, I imagined, to the way he was before he slashed his fingers, after leaving Cabresi's orchestra. He was on a high, but it would go too far. He'd be furious suddenly. Cause some scene. Get into a row with someone, start to shout the odds. He challenged everyone, and at every opportunity – the hypocrisy he saw around him, the shallowness of this existence. As if it wasn't his. His purpose was not always to speak as he found, but to wound.

I was as bad as the rest of them, I made money out of people like him. Crippled people. I didn't care. I wanted to control him, I thought my way better than his. He started missing sessions. Just not turning up. Then he'd storm into the next one and tell some hideous story, the reason he hadn't made it, throwing it at me like a challenge: he hadn't woken up in time, he'd been to a party the night before, some girl who was there, he'd gone home and fucked her . . .

I lower myself into my bath.

I look at my body. I think, Somehow the bodily functions of babies are undisturbing. Their morning breath, phlegmy throats, excreta smelling like a warning in the crease of their nappies, are not offensive. How? As though the older we get the more polluted our insides, leaking outside. Crusty eyes, weeping after a night's sleep, sweat masked over with deodorant, flaking scalps in greasy hair . . . I have read that when the doors of a plane are opened after a long-haul flight those on the other side cover their noses and mouths against the stench that erupts from within. The living wash themselves in vain.

Twenty-nine

But let me just lie here, just let me lie here forever. I could lose my edges then, I could lose my form. My mind might come with me under water, thought might switch off, restricted to this space. If I could stop thinking of him . . .

But I've been thinking of him for so many years that to stop would make them seem a waste. I continue in folly to give my foolish past validity. So depressingly predictable.

We'd meet on a Monday and a Thursday. Thursdays were usually fine, we made headway. Thursdays left me hopeful, positive, benign. But on Mondays he might not turn up, or he might but he wouldn't have slept, or he'd say something mean, cruel, that glint in his eye, my connection with him would vanish.

I made up excuses for him. All that had happened. I

rewound every step of the way: this anger, this needing to prove . . . His parents, Cabresi, his college days, Lizzie . . . 'I was so good,' he'd once said to me, 'that Cabresi employed me before I'd finished studying,' and he'd started late, incredible really . . . His failed career. And James. Obviously James. James is the one who buys drugs, James doles them out, James picks his moment.

I find myself hating him, blaming him, taking things personally, waging a mental war; it becomes a question of beating him – my way over his way – I see him with Lee, it hurts, why does it hurt? Why does it hurt to picture them together?

In the quiet of my flat one day, naked in my bath, I know it for what it is. I feel left out. I feel possessive. Their friendship exists, ours doesn't. I'm jealous.

How had he done it? Who is he anyway? Just some bloke with a chip on his shoulder. Moody, unreliable, self-absorbed. Endlessly sensitive but only as far as himself; not a genius with a tragic flaw, just flawed, nothing to him but his story.

In my mind I took him apart. I took myself apart, too. I'd crossed a line – I didn't know how but I'd crossed it. Working out why, although my professional credo, was less important than acting on this. I thought I'd better not see him, tell him to find someone else, say I believed we'd gone as far as we could go . . . I had to cut him out.

Thirty

This thought comes back to me. This thought worries me. I felt like this again not long before he died. If he had lived, would it have carried on happening? More and more often, perhaps, the periods lengthening each time. Would I have disliked him in the end? Had nothing to do with him finally? Got on with my life, like Bob, like Cabresi?

I'll put on some music, some Bach, I save it for moments like these. The feeling it stirs up within me, wonderful torture, cutting right through me, letting me see him again; he's tall, his legs are strong, the top half of his body flows freely, his feet support him squarely on the ground, he is made for the cello, he played these cello suites. Dances, apparently, though I can't see how anyone could dance as slowly as that. Slow and melancholy. In the simplicity of note following note, soft, then louder, low, then soaring, the piano walking slowly underneath, they seem to contain everything poignant, everything hopeful, all the sadness of the world. He was warm and attractive and passionate, he was full. There were so many things you'd imagine he'd be, so much at his disposal. He hooked me.

As all those years ago he hooked Cabresi; as now he'd hook Gina . . .

I didn't stop seeing him. I took on the challenge. I thought, My reactions have nothing to do with anyone else, I am the one who should change, then I might help him. See how my mind played tricks? I fooled myself I'd get him out of my system without getting him out of my life . . . As though a few strict words to myself were enough to persuade me. Deconstruct him: he isn't worth it; deconstruct yourself: your behaviour is ridiculous.

Nevertheless, I believed we'd reached an impasse, that my

days had resumed their anodyne normality. I congratulated myself on the battle fought and won, the struggle with emotion, the semi-madness – it seemed now – calmed down. I'd righted myself, restored the balance. Did I care? Not as much. Euphoria when I saw him? Gone. Misery when he didn't turn up? Gone too. Good ... But then he met Gina.

Thirty-one

He'd nearly finished the house. Two years, but it had been worth it. All that was left now were odds and ends, finishing touches. He thought he'd done a good job. He'd got work on the back of it. He was pleased. James was putting a lodger in with him, slightly annoying ... Some girl from Cornwall. A family friend. The daughter of a woman who used to babysit when she was a teenager, a young girl, early twenties.

He wasn't looking forward to it. He'd got used to living on his own. Besides which, he'd feel uncomfortable sharing a house with someone so much younger, like he might shock her, or be a bad influence; like he might find her immature.

But he loved Gina the moment he met her. That's the way I expected he'd be, that's the way he always was at first, undiscriminating, taking people in, thinking they were great, then tearing them to shreds when he realized that they weren't. His friendships were played out on the town, that was their forum. They struck up in bars and at parties, they deepened on the dancefloors of nightclubs, they flared up with drink, quietened down, and moved on.

Gina was there all the time. Gina was different, generous and sweet, she made him see things in another light. He felt protective towards her – not that she wasn't independent. Not that she didn't go out; she did, but without an agenda. She'd go out for fun. She didn't need to impress, or get trashed or have the best time ever, he'd say – as though this concept was an alien one.

All of a sudden women start worrying him. The way he relates to them, views them, someone's given him books on the subject, self-help books, and he's started to see himself inside their pages. He'd put his recent attitude down to his depression, to what happened that night with Lara and Lizzie but now he's wondering whether that night with Lara and Lizzie happened because of his attitude. His picking up of women in bars, the casual nature of the interaction, his temper with them in the morning, his rush to get them gone, to obliterate all evidence of their encounter, it's not so new. He behaved this way after he and Lizzie split up – which you could put down to a broken heart but – he behaved this way before he met Liz – which you could put down to youth. But why was he different with her, then? Was it that she matched him blow for blow? Why was he different with Lara? Was it that he couldn't get her? There's a certain anger, or is it fear? He's always been nastiest to the nicest ones. Why is that? Where does it come from? Is it something to do with Nancy?

I should have been happy, I suppose, relieved at his progress. But part of me thought, You're right to be afraid. Love is the biggest destabilizing influence. All those hideous acts of terrorism, selfishness, desperation, jealousy committed with 'I love you' on the lips, the letting someone in under your armour, the terrible journey back to yourself afterwards. I thought, Therapy, like religion, is just a form of socialization, I thought, Deconstruction is not always a useful tool . . .

See how my mind played tricks? I thought, the Age of Therapy, the Age of Information, too much information. It's not enough to have a feeling, you have to quantify it, pin it onto something else, route it backwards. Freedom just to act, though . . . I prepared myself for my descent . . . I began to forbid analysis.

Thirty-two

Friday nights he always went out with James. Their evenings followed a regular pattern: start off in a bar, then move to another, maybe collecting people they knew or people they didn't along the way, maybe tagging along to something else that's going on, an opening, a party, a club where they're on the guest list. At some point, they always went to the Orange Room, the Orange Room was failsafe. If there was nothing else happening after closing time, it would still be open, if they hadn't met anyone interesting anywhere else, they would there, they were known there . . .

I remember the Monday he came to see me, a different expression on his face. He'd been out on Friday as usual with James. They'd bumped into a girl they vaguely knew and followed her off to some bar. Her name was Zoë. She said she was a singer/songwriter.

Lee challenged her to a demonstration but she said it

was too early for that and he'd better stick around. He told her he had no intention of doing anything else. She was a mixed-race girl, quite pretty, close-cropped hair, a compact, muscular body and a strong desire, it transpired over the course of the evening, to wind him up. She was in her element on that stool by the bar, head held high, flirting with both of them in this clever-clever way, hurling their conversation back at them – witty, she probably liked to think. 'You really reckon you're something,' said Lee.

'Then we've got something in common,' she said.

She was mates with some bloke called Col, who turned up at that point and she flung her arms round his neck. He said, 'All right?'

He was nice, Col, no bullshit, Lee knew him a little. He was on his way to a party and invited them to tag along. 'I'm not up for it,' said Lee.

'Someone give him a line,' said James.

'Yes,' said Zoë, 'I've got some. Help yourself.'

He didn't know how long they stayed there, three more pints perhaps, a couple of trips to the toilet with Zoë's wrap; she was good for something, then; it made him laugh that James held onto his.

At the party he fell into conversation with two Danish girls over on holiday. They had ended up at the party by mistake. They were cousins, tall and blonde, he fancied them both, he decided. High, pleasantly drunk, out in some stranger's house, he didn't know where exactly, two beautiful women, he didn't know which one he wanted, he felt incredibly lucky, suddenly, like he lived the best life ever, like he was amazingly charmed. All that he had, all that he was became clear to him, in this place, with these people, laughing, joking, two stunning women, taking his pick—

Zoë came over. 'I've been watching you,' she said.

She got on his nerves. She turned everything he said into a joke; collected his words, chewed them up and spat them out at him as evidence that he was an idiot. 'Why don't you piss off?' he said.

'And leave these girls at your mercy?'

She began to ingratiate herself with them by flattering them, their hair, their clothes, then talking to them in languages Lee didn't understand, French, German; she made some comment which set them off laughing, obviously concerning him, he said, 'You're a witch.'

'You're right, I am.'

'You're a psycho.'

In the middle of the room he saw James doing that weird dance of his, sort of slithering up and down, his eyes closed. Lee went over to him. He said, 'I'm heading off.'

But somehow all six of them were in the street together, maybe Zoë had collected up Col and her two new friends and followed them out. 'Where are we going?' asked one of the Danish girls.

'Fuck it,' said Col. 'That's enough for me.'

'We could go to the Orange Room,' said James.

'We'd have to get two cabs.'

'So?'

'Okay,' said Lee, 'you go with Zoë, I'll meet you there.'

'No,' said Zoë, 'you boys go together.'

'Whatever,' said Lee.

She was already there when they arrived, dancing provocatively with the other two girls. She beckoned him over but he shook his head and bought a vodka tonic. James told him he'd left him a line in the toilet. He went to get it, smiling to himself. What a nightmare that girl was – but she was obviously up for it. The floor, the walls, the colours around him pulsated brightly in and out like a bouncy castle, him a little kid in the middle, it wouldn't matter which way he fell. There were three cubicles in these toilets, the one on the right had a windowsill above the cistern, white tiles, you wouldn't see a line of coke unless you were looking. He laughed. James was so tight. He didn't know anyone who didn't just hand over the wrap, who kept his coke a secret if someone else had some. There was the line in the corner. It was a fat one. James must be wasted, he thought, and laughed again.

Back in the room Lee saw him leaning against the bar talking to Gina, of all people. He smiled and waved. He went over. James was making no sense at all, he was sweating, his body had a quality of chewing gum about it, boneless, long. 'Having fun?' Lee grinned, but she wasn't eager to hug him. She had an expression – he couldn't place it – on her face. He said, 'What?' and she chewed the air at him grotesquely. He realized he was gurning, he put his hand to his jaw, he clenched his teeth together.

'Who are they?' she asked, pointing at Zoë and the Danish girls dancing away. No one else was.

'Friends of mine,' he said angrily. 'All right?'

He went over to join them. Got right in the middle and began to dance, he loved to dance, he closed his eyes. Zoë was good, he'd noticed. He looked again. Yeah, she could move. Perhaps she wasn't so bad after all, at least she knew how to have a laugh. She didn't care what anyone thought, she did what she wanted. She caught his eye and winked and turned her body to him, swayed it, this way, that way, right down low, her mouth close to his groin. He laughed to himself. Maybe he liked her style.

When he sat down, she sat on his knee. He said, 'I thought I was an idiot.'

'I'm just looking after them.'

'You what?'

'Those girls. They're friends. You were coming between them.'

'Here we go.'

'You were going to choose one and make the other hate her. You're such a misogynist.'

'And you're a nightmare.'

'I thought I'd put myself in the firing line.'

'That's good of you,' he said, and kissed her.

After that the evening dissolved. He remembered Zoë singing some song, standing on a table, James dancing for hours in a corner, one of the Danish girls crying, Gina saying goodbye. He woke up not in his bed, Zoë beside him.

It wasn't an unusual Saturday morning but he had an unusual feeling. He was too hungover to know what it was. He got up and found her bathroom. He stepped under the shower, he felt like shit. Cringing skin, nausea, and not just physical. He shivered a little, turned up the hot water. He didn't usually feel embarrassed like this. That's what it was. Embarrassment.

It got worse on his way back home. It was the prospect of Gina, he realized. He realized he was ashamed that she'd seen him last night, like that, it surprised him. He didn't feel it on account of Zoë or James or any of the witnesses there'd been on countless other evenings. That was who he was. Only, he wasn't with Gina. Apart from James, Gina was the one person he didn't know from going out. If he thought about it, apart from James he counted her his closest friend. She saw him all the time, she knew what he was really like. Then, if he was ashamed, the way he had behaved last night, it wasn't really him. Was it? His head was spinning.

She was out at work when he got back. She must have gone somewhere else after that because she hadn't returned by the time he went to bed. On Sunday morning he got up and started cooking bacon. Gina appeared in her dressing gown. She said, 'Lovely smell to wake up to,' and smiled. Nothing seemed to have changed. They ate it in front of the telly, one either end of the sofa. She said nothing about it. Neither did he.

All day, though, he was itching to mention it, scenes from Friday night kept flashing through his mind, making him squirm and screw up his face. Finally he brought it up. He said, 'Was I a mess?'

She laughed. She said, 'With that hideous girl.'

'She isn't that bad.'

'And your nose bright red from coke, chewing your teeth.'

'Really?' he grimaced.

'It's not a look.'

He'd liked that.

*   *   *

He has a different expression on his face as he tells me the story. Suddenly, like a threadworm a thought goes through me. One thought, quicker than lightning, thin end of the wedge, undoing all my rebalancing. Lee and James falling out, making room for Gina.

Thirty-three

I thought it, but I never imagined this end: Gina and James together, Lee dead.

I thought it and I was in again, I had a vested interest. This time, though, it didn't catch me unawares. I noticed it. I wrestled for a minute. I thought, This isn't healthy. Then I wondered why. I wondered what to do. That's when I must have decided. That's when I let things go. I thought, Perhaps the only experience worth having is an intense experience, and, I'm not going to analyse this, just act.

Ironically, he started to invent all sorts of psychotherapeutic reasons for the way he behaved. It was Nancy. She was at the heart of it. See, he'd heard that if a child was loved for his abilities he always had to prove himself, but if he was loved for just who he was, he didn't – it was an insecurity thing. Nancy loved him to perform ... Slowly it started clicking into place. He'd been loved for being larger than life – on the football field, in the school play, entertaining Nancy in the kitchen – and in his head he'd associated those two things, cause and effect: I perform, I receive love. Not literally performing. Not playing the cello. Playing the fool, playing up, going out and being outrageous. Love me, I'm the life and the soul of the party.

He was giving it a rest for a while. He was going to get his head straight. He didn't want any more crazy nights from which it took him three days to recover. He wondered what ill-effects they were having on his state of mind. He'd felt pretty calm recently, but there'd been a period before Gina moved in when he'd lurched from one extreme to another – euphoria, anger, cynicism, hope – it was exhausting; he wanted to empty out, he wanted to know who he was, no external stimulus.

I watched him. I knew that feeling.

I began actively to involve myself, react to Lee, take things out of my head and put them in his. He'd talk about women, I'd tell him how perfect James had been for him – the companionship of a sexual relationship without its emotional demands. I'd say James held back his personal development. I paid more attention when he talked about Gina . . . Gina was my hope just as Lizzie was Cabresi's.

Thirty-four

It was lovely, the house Lee rebuilt. Nothing ostentatious. The front door opened onto a staircase in a large, open room. French windows at the back looked onto the garden. The kitchen was where the bathroom used to be, a substantial glass extension added on. Above it was an office, all windows and skylights, a right-angled desk built into the wall. The new bathroom was a bedroom converted. Free-standing tub, white walls, blue mosaic on the floor. Up some steps was Gina's bedroom. Right next door was Lee's. It was a sunny house, small but open, light but private. He'd got work on the back of it. People who'd come round, you know how it is, one thing leads to another, word spreads. He'd laid floors, fitted kitchens, painted and decorated. Quite boring, painting and decorating.

But he was feeling really happy like he hadn't in a long time, like maybe he never had before. He felt content. He loved his little house, he felt he'd made it, created something out of nothing very nice, he'd never known this feeling.

The past year had been his very lowest. Not while he was still unwell, but when he was supposedly better. Living in the house after the initial excitement of the project had worn off, those miserable rooms, freezing bathroom, dirty kitchen, his bedroom, musty, stuffy, damp – that smelly old mattress; then the building site the house became, in retrospect it had really depressed him, he was sure he'd gone out so much because he couldn't bear to be at home. Recently he'd noticed how different things were, how happy he was, like something pressing on him had been taken off, like he was lighter. The house was pretty much done. It was summer. He'd been thinking about the garden. He didn't know anything about gardens and neither did Gina, but she'd said, 'How hard can it be? You buy something, you plant it . . .' He thought he might turn his hand to outside. Inside, the only thing needing attention was the loft conversion, it was going to be great. But the lights weren't in, he hadn't done the floor or any decorating, water was getting in somewhere, he didn't know where, it was dripping through to Gina's bedroom.

Last Saturday night he'd woken to find her standing in his doorway. She said, 'Can I get in?'

He was shocked at first, sleepy, confused. She said, 'Water's been pouring on my bed.'

She'd moved it to the middle of the room but her mattress and duvet were wet, a steady drip continued from the ceiling into a bucket she'd put underneath. She said, 'I was dreaming I was drowning.'

'This is my fault.'

'It isn't.'

'I wonder where it's coming in?'

'You can't look now.'

'No, in the morning.'

'Can I get in with you, then?'

'Okay.'

'You don't mind?'

'Why should I?'

Under their dressing gowns they realized they had nothing on and he went to get a pair of pants while she put on a tee shirt. He got into his bed, plumped up the pillows on her side and waited for her to come back. He felt strangely embarrassed. He felt sure she did too. Downstairs, during the daytime, their relationship was tactile – he was always throwing his arms around her, or she snuggling in beside him on the settee. Somehow under the duvet he felt exposed. She got in next to him. They lay there in the darkness saying nothing, each knowing the other stayed awake. He slept fitfully, uncomfortably, woke often feeling anxious, he was tired and irritable and grumpy when his alarm eventually rang.

In the morning he went up on the roof and saw some slates had fallen off. There was a gap in the floorboards of the loft that went through to Gina's ceiling. He'd have to get new slates and then he'd have to mend the roof, he wasn't sure how long it would take him. He thought he'd put some plastic down in the meantime. But he didn't do it immediately, and then he didn't get round to it, and it was just his luck that as soon as it got dark it started raining again, and he had to spend another night in bed with Gina.

This time, though, things were completely different. A complacency had settled upon her, as though one night was enough to form a habit. Usually when they went to bed they did so at different times, or else the evening would end on the landing, one waiting in their bedroom until the other had finished in the bathroom. Tonight she followed him up the stairs joking and laughing, continued her conversation while he was cleaning his teeth, popped in and out in varying states of undress, then hung her dressing gown on the back of his door vaguely bossily, it made him laugh. She got in. She said, 'What?' He didn't want anything to break the mood, he thought he might embarrass her if he referred to their situation there in bed so he said, 'Nothing,' and changed the subject. They carried on chatting once the lights were out. At some point, they must have fallen asleep.

Next day he started a painting and decorating job, so he ordered the slates for the roof but didn't get around to putting down the plastic. The weather had changed anyway, he doubted it would rain, but Gina seemed reluctant to put

it to the test. 'Well, I'll definitely do it at the weekend,'
he said.

'Shall I just stay with you till then?'

'If you like.'

'Okay.'

She was asleep when he came in on Friday. He'd been
out somewhere with James, but it wasn't late. He'd looked
forward to coming back, returning and finding her there, in
bed already. He'd had a bit to drink, he was feeling friendly,
he climbed in on her side and cuddled her awake. He said,
'You're so cosy.'

She got comfortable beside him, put her legs through
his and her hands to his chest. She said, 'It's nice sleeping
like this.'

Saturday, though, he put up the plastic sheeting. Gina
was at work so he left her a note. He collected the slates.
He thought he might as well finish the job, so he went
up to the roof in the afternoon and hammered them on,
then filled in the gaps of the floorboards in the loft. Now
he was here, he might as well sand this floor. He might as
well give the walls an undercoat. He might as well paint
the patch on Gina's ceiling where the water came in. He
ended up working all evening. Made a bit of supper, had
an early night.

He was startled awake by Gina getting into bed beside
him. He sat up suddenly. He said,

'Gina—'

'Hello.'

'The leak's fixed. I left you a note.'

'It's four in the morning, my bedroom's topsy-turvy.'

'I'm not wearing any clothes.'

'So?'

'Have you had a drink?'

'I'm not wearing any clothes either.' She pulled his arm around her, nothing more, she went to sleep.

She stayed after that. She never went back to her room. It was only to be another two weeks that she lived in the house, but she didn't move back to her room.

Thirty-five

I should go to my room. I should go to bed. Look at me here, shivering in my towel—

It can't have been my fault, can it, this turn of events? This new friendship of Lee's which would lead to a souring of that other one? I didn't think James would play dirty.

But didn't I? Wasn't it obvious? Wasn't I looking forward to the drama of it? To casting him out, bringing him down? (Perhaps he'll be brought down tomorrow.)

The way we all fought with him! The way we all battled for Lee. Cabresi, Lizzie, me – even Gina now – which of us wouldn't have known that James would fight back?

Even Gina now, although in a small way, although in a small, perhaps subconscious way. Lee's falling out with James wasn't wholly down to her but she proved a willing ingredient; the situation was just too dynamic to leave it alone. That strange connection they had, coming between them, blowing it to smithereens.

'We were talking about Lizzie,' he said to me. 'I don't know how it came up. Gina said, "James told me you always went out on a Friday night and you didn't take her. Why not?" kind of thing, and "Didn't she mind?" I said, "I didn't take her because James didn't want her along, he was always rude to her," she said, "Why?" "I don't think he likes women much," I said, and she said, "That's funny, that's what he says about you." Then it turns out that when she moved in James said, "Lee's really hard to live with, I won't blame you if it doesn't work." I know this sounds petty but it's rattled me, I always thought it was me and him, I always thought I could trust him.'

'Yes,' I said.

And then very seriously, 'If he says that sort of thing to Gina, what's he saying to everyone else?'

He paused for a long time. He looked at me. Slowly he said, 'Exactly.'

Thirty-six

It was the first time I'd sniffed doubt in him. I wondered how he'd cope. It was all coming at once, his decision to stop going out so much, his deepening involvement with Gina, his footing with James slipping away. But the next time I saw him he'd rationalized. He said, 'So James said that, so what? It was taken out of context. It might have been a joke . . . And anyway it's bollocks. I get on great with women. I love women. Gina says I'm her perfect flatmate.'

They began to spend more time together. Now he was taking things easier he went out with her instead of with James. They'd go for a drink in the evenings or round to a friend's or out to a film. At the weekends they'd cook a big

lunch then lounge in the garden all afternoon. They hadn't
got far with the gardening. But he made a bench and a table
out of breeze blocks and wood, he'd built a barbecue, he'd
even put up an outside light.

He didn't seem to think it was strange that for the past
two weeks they'd been getting into bed together, that it
didn't look like this was a temporary thing. But he didn't
want to go into it, he batted my questions away as though
wondering about a future might endanger the present. That
was my interpretation. He didn't mind telling me about it
but he didn't like to analyse, that I understood. He found
it funny the way she'd got bossy with his body, the way
she arranged it around her until she was comfy, until she
was totally nestled in. I asked him to describe it. He said
they faced the same way. His stomach in the small of her
back, the front of his knees in the arch of hers, his left arm
around her, his left hand holding her right, his right hand
holding her left, his right arm either under her neck or over
the top of her head, he couldn't think which, it had always
been uncomfortable with everyone else, but it wasn't with
her. I said, 'Don't you want to make love to her?'

He said, 'She's like my sister.'

Thirty-seven

'Does James know you sleep together?' I couldn't help asking.

'No.'

'What will he do when he does?'

'What do you mean?'

I didn't answer.

Thirty-eight

How much of this was down to me? Lee took things at
face value but I prompted him to look for subtext. As he
started to spend more time with Gina he spent less time
with James and James reacted. Lee found it funny. He'd
say to me, 'James is always ringing me, three times a day
sometimes, sometimes with nothing to say . . . He's really
getting on my nerves.'

But I said, 'He hates it that you're getting a life. He's
panicking.

I said, 'I wonder if he'll do anything else.'

'Like what?'

'Well he's always kept you to himself somehow. He came
between you and your peers, you and Cabresi, you and
Lizzie . . . What will he do to you and Gina?'

'No,' he said eventually, 'you're wrong. He was there for
me. When I was ill he kept me alive. If I'd been on my own,
or had to pay rent – he looked after me.'

'Well,' I said, 'some people are fantastic nurses –
it doesn't necessarily mean that they're kind. Perhaps
illness makes them feel strong, powerful, healthy, perhaps James felt whole next to someone broken like
you.'

Our time was up.

Thirty-nine

Little by little, comments of mine trickled into him and
came out of his mouth as his own. James had him on a

string, Lee hated himself for not having noticed before. 'I've been thinking about something you said. Something you said about people who look after you. Not necessarily being kind but because of the power. I remembered a comment of James's. It was when I was ill, living with him, getting better, I said to him once, "Will you do me a favour?" wanting some small thing, like, pass that record, and he came back at me with, "Every day I do you a favour," it stuck in my mind. It was a joke – but you'd say there was no such thing. And maybe you're right. Maybe it *was* all to do with power for him. Making me live in that building site – that old man's mattress! He could've given me some cash for that.'

If he picked it apart he couldn't say why he was friends with James. If he met him for the first time today would he like him? What did James have in his favour? All their friendship had was history. James was easy to be with because he'd been there so much it was like he wasn't there at all. He was a habit, a prop – like some people can't go to a party without a cigarette, Lee couldn't go without James. He was his buffer.

He did what James wanted, mostly unconsciously, went where James felt like, kept him sweet, why did he do it?

They were so different. Poles apart, even Gina said, in every way. 'If you saw us together, Peter, you'd know what I mean. Gina was laughing about it the other day. She said, "You're such an unnatural couple," and we are. I'm not explaining myself right. If only you could see him.'

I almost said, forgetfully, 'But I have seen him,' but

I managed to bite my tongue. It wasn't appropriate to mention it. Last week, the week before perhaps, I'd been in town and wandered past a bar whose name I recognized. Lee had mentioned it, it suddenly occurred to me, in a couple of our previous sessions, and I wondered if it was unethical to go inside. I went in anyway. It was new, only recently opened, it had an air of arrogance and hope; a retro yet futuristic feel to it, the futuristic chic of a bygone age. I ordered a gin martini and looked about me. What would happen, I wondered, if Lee walked in? I felt almost sick for a moment, a mixture of terror and excitement, then I realized that he wouldn't. It was Tuesday. He played football on a Tuesday. Still, perhaps he knew these people, perhaps I'd heard him talk in detail about that man over there or that woman there, perhaps one of these people was James? I looked more closely. A couple of the men fitted James's description. A third one coming out of the toilet could easily be him. Someone called and it *was* him. I was thrilled. It was a tiny stab of power.

Forty

It's the same in the courtroom, occasionally. It buoys me up, from time to time, putting faces to names . . . But it's quickly replaced by that other, more desolate feeling. Like attending a funeral full of old friends and suddenly knowing. The only one you want to see is the dead one . . .

I surprise myself with the extent of my mourning. A year on and I still catch myself crying in the middle of some mundane task. I wonder, does this mean I loved him? When he was alive it was the same. Do I love him? I met him at least twice a week for over five years, that's a habit to break—

But two fifty-minute meetings in a week. One hundred minutes out of the ten thousand and eighty available. Not even one per cent. Nought point nine nine two . . .

When he wasn't there, though, I conjured him. In the evenings, in my flat, I'd stop what I was doing, or save him up for later, like a treat – I knew it was foolish, I couldn't help it. I'd lie in bed as I'm lying now, assume this posture, body relaxed, eyes closed, hands folded softly over heart; I breathed deeply, I thought about Lee. It gave me pleasure.

I'd imagine him in bed with Gina. The beautiful strangeness of their routine, platonic, sensual; slipping slowly into something else—

'I kissed her on the back of the neck this morning.'

'What did she say?'

'She said, do it again.'

'Don't you find her attractive?'

'I'm trying to build a friendship with her.'

'Don't you want to make love to her?'

'I just think of all the reasons why not.'

'Why not?'

I was dying to know what she looked like. I knew she worked in a restaurant-bar, I knew where it was, I was glad it was the other end of town. Otherwise curiosity might well have got in the way of integrity and I would have gone there. But what would be wrong in that? I couldn't really answer my own question though I batted it around from time to time. In the end it was like reaching for a cigarette once you've given up. It was like smoking the whole thing even though it tasted horrible, telling yourself it tasted horrible and you'd never do it again, knowing you were hooked.

It was early Saturday morning and there was only one other person in there. I almost had Gina all to myself. I ordered two poached eggs and she wrote this down while I watched her hands around the pen. I imagined them holding Lee's hands. She had short dark hair (I was surprised by this) and the same blue-grey eyes as he did; she had lovely skin. As I left I felt happy. I could see them together and they looked good.

Forty-one

I could imagine James lying in his bed, in his flat just around the corner from his house, his house that now looked much nicer than his flat, alone in his bed while Lee was in bed with Gina. I could imagine the workings of his mind, the irritant thoughts that made him curl his toes, turn over, twist himself up in his sheets. Lee was overtaking him. That house, that girl, that line of work that gave him satisfaction; making something. Lee finding his feet, finding a life, not so many boys' nights out, what would James do then? The horrid emptiness of his world, his business, selling space, selling nothing, making only money, his home, nothing to come back to, time he spent there in the evenings was time spent alone. But Lee was with Gina. Gina was my hope.

Forty-two

Just as Lizzie was Cabresi's – but how foolish of us. Lee always regarded women with a certain scorn. At base he did.

Feminism he took as a personal insult. 'Why do you want to be men?' he screamed at Gina at the party he gave for her. 'It's coming back on you because we don't want you. Men don't want women like you.' In the end, everything happened because of that party.

Forty-three

But it wasn't his fault, really. It wasn't wholly his. There were so many factors contributing to the evening. There was James. James telling Gina to be careful of Lee; Gina telling Lee James said this; James bringing Lara to the party; James ringing Tony . . . It was James. James brought the two things that he knew would shake Lee up, he brought Lara and he brought cocaine, and then he left. He set the dominoes falling.

Forty-four

In a way James was delightfully predictable, I just didn't predict he'd win. When he found out that Lee and Gina were sharing a bed, he started taking Gina to one side. He talked to her earnestly, everything he said got back. He said, 'What's going to happen when Lee gets a girlfriend? I don't want you getting hurt.'

'He's the sort of man who can make a girl go mad. I know. I've seen it.'

'You only know seventy per cent of Lee. You've never seen him off his head.'

For some reason, this last comment hurt him. He came to the conclusion it was because it was true, the way he was out on the town embarrassed him, he was ashamed of taking drugs. He knew they blurred his faculties, knew what they turned him into but he couldn't resist them. I said, 'That habit you've got into, though, that way of socializing, has been formed with James. He's the one who first gave you cocaine, he's the one you went out with all the time. He took you on those self-destructive binges after you left the orchestra, he tempted you out again when your breakdown forced you to give it all up. You want to know why you did what James wanted, went where he felt like, "kept him sweet"? It was coke. James gave you coke. If there's a monster he's created it.'

I paused. I wondered what effect my outburst would have. He was quiet for a moment, he looked at me.

'Yes,' he said. 'The scenes I caused sometimes, the dramas, the fights, James revelled in all that. Being outrageous, pissing everyone off. He never had the guts to do it himself. He'd say, "I've left you a line in the toilet," and I'd go and take it . . . In the toilet, though, on top of the cistern, on the windowsill if there was one. Sometimes someone else would have got it. That's the risk he would take. Not even the wrap. So he could control my intake. So he could control the way I behaved.'

He began to look at his life. His periods of greatest unhappiness were when James was integral: following the accident; after he left the orchestra; when he broke up with Lizzie; while he was at college . . . Didn't I think it was weird that while he was *there* nobody liked him, but as soon as he left and James wasn't around he got on fine with his peers? He'd been happiest when James hadn't been so important: when things were good with Lizzie; when all was well in the orchestra. Now he was getting things together, getting content, and now James was taking a back seat.

But what had the attraction been, how had it continued? He knew it sounded snobbish, but James was ... so much less than him – less friendly, less attractive, less talented, how had it happened that they'd got so close? It was like he'd fallen out of love suddenly and violently, he wanted to understand his former viewpoint, he wanted excuse. Having picked apart the most enduring and important relationship in his life and found nothing at its core, he wanted to know how he'd been able to construct it in the first place. He remembered the past as he never had before. With clarity he recalled his early college days. 'Do you see how he got me?' he said, 'Do you see how he did it?'

He had no need to point it out.

Forty-five

It was the moment I'd been waiting for. The moment stayed with me. I was happy then, so happy. It was summer I remember. One evening after work was over, I decided to walk for a while before catching my bus. Walking on air. Everyone I passed seemed cheerful, everyone out and about. It occurred to me that it was Friday night.

It was always Friday it felt like, you woke up on Monday morning and before you knew it the week was over. You woke up, took a breath and it was lunchtime. How did that happen? Days hurtled into one another in this city.

This is so many people's city, it amused me to imagine it as Lee's. To see it through his eyes, as he'd defined it, his possession, his patch. I found myself walking in the direction he might walk, down this road towards the centre of town, past these pubs spilling out on the street, those cafés with their tables on the pavement. I found myself walking towards the Orange Room.

This was where they used to come to, always, without fail. So monotonous, I never understood the attraction. Ever since I'd met Lee, Friday nights had been sacred to James and at some point they'd come to the Orange Room, but now he'd met Gina. Tonight he was doing something else with her.

It must have been five years since I'd been there in the evening. These days, I sometimes went for lunch but that was all. I looked around me. Everyone looked familiar. The same types who'd been there when I was a frequent punter a decade earlier. Same people, different clothes. I ordered a gin martini and the man standing next to me said, 'That's a good idea. I'll have one of those.

'Sorry,' he said, 'I didn't mean to offend you. You look appalled!'

'No,' I said, 'it's not that—' it was James.

'What?'

'You reminded me of someone, you surprised me. I've come to my senses now.'

We stood together while the barman fixed our drinks, my head buzzing with an over excitement. He started talking to me. Told me his name, asked mine, asked me if I came here much, I said no, not any more, I didn't like it, he made a joke, I quipped back, that kind of thing . . . All the time, certain I must have a massive grin on my face, can feel myself smiling; right behind my eyes can feel Lee. Feel like his life has become for me some weird reality, like a movie I knew by heart and then stepped into. All the time talking to this man, smiling at him, sharing a joke, thinking I know all about him, he doesn't have a clue. Those little round eyes, sly eyes, smiling at me, the tricks he's pulled, the wraps left in the toilet, the manipulation, the power games, the chip chip chipping away at Lee's confidence, can you tell just by looking at him? Maybe you can.

Forty-six

The following Thursday was Gina's birthday. Lee had only found out when he heard a message on the answerphone, and berated her for not telling him herself. 'Oh,' she said, 'it's no big deal. I'm going to Cornwall the next day anyway.'

'I'll drive you down if you like.'

'You want to come?'

'You wouldn't have to get the train.'

'I'd love you to come.'

'We could take Thursday and Friday off. Do something really nice on Thursday—'

'We could.'

'—then drive down Friday during the day. If I'm bullying you tell me to fuck off.'

He told me all this in therapy the Monday before they were due to leave. He thought he might get some people round on Wednesday evening, have a bit of a birthday bash. 'Will you invite James?' I asked.

'I've got to,' he said. 'And whatever I might think, he *was* there for me, he did give me a job, somewhere to live – in a way, he's given me Gina.'

'Yes,' I said. 'Well. If someone gives you all that they can also take it away.'

'How?' said Lee. 'He can't take Gina, she doesn't believe the things he says. He can't take my job. He could take the house back but I can always find another place to live. What can he take then?'

All these things, as it turned out.

PART THREE

PART THREE

One

I am in the club that night because Lee has asked me to be there. I was already busy seeing Joseph but Lee said, 'That doesn't matter, bring him along.' He's a young boy, Joseph, and sweet, but he's got an air of Lee about him, that fascination with things that don't matter, places to be seen in, people to know. He's just starting out, he's a baby, he's wide-eyed and impressed and he's never been anywhere before. He's shy. I could eat him up.

The Orange Room comes up in conversation. I can tell that he's eager to go. 'Okay,' I say, and he looks all nervous and excited, 'there's nothing special about it. It's just a place like any other.'

James is at the bar – the blood goes to my head. He says, 'In here again, Peter? I thought you hated this place.'

I say, 'I do. But Joseph and I were just having dinner and he said he'd never been here before.'

Joseph blushes.

Lee arrives. Seemingly out of his head with anger. He comes over to James and pushes a finger and thumb under his jaw. He says, 'You've gone too far this time.' Shouts—

But then he turns on me. He didn't do this. He shouts, '*You've* gone too far.'

I say, 'Not me.'

'You,' he repeats.

'You,' says James.

'You,' nods Joseph. I look from face to face.

I say, 'This isn't how it happens ...' I say, 'Not me.' Everyone crowds in. I scream. I wake up.

Always the same. Each day like a birth. I scream. I fill my lungs. I wake up.

Two

I lie still for a moment. Reality trickles back. Behind the curtains, light waits.

Fate waits. James's fate decided today ... But in this gap before today has started, in this space of not-quite-yet, in bed, it could almost be that none of it has happened, all of it was dreams, Lee is still alive.

I have his details in my phone book, I call up him from time to time. A voice says, '*Sorry, this number is currently unavailable.*' Currently.

The finality of it slowly trickles in, each day a little more, like that light through my curtains. Perhaps when I realize, then perhaps, I'll wake up without first thinking of him, without first feeling sorrow; dreading the day. I switch on the radio and the world opens out. Reassuring voices reading the news, talking to all of us emerging from our duvets or already on the road, driving to work. The comfort of routine.

The task ahead. The clothes left on the chair ready for me to fill them, the visit to the bathroom, the perfunctory cup of coffee, the bus ride to the courtroom ...

Three

I am familiar with the journey now, a regular along this bus route. Often I see the same old faces and I wonder if they recognize mine. How do our days compare? Would they ever imagine my macabre destination, the nature of the hours I spend, the same story over and over, the life of this man, this death? Why should they? In my head, I try to change places.

Into my head flashes his face. He's grinning. He's saying, 'I thought I might get some people round on Wednesday evening, have a bit of a birthday bash.'

'Will you invite James?' I ask.

'I've got to,' he says.

Almost as soon as he mentions it I foresee disaster ahead. Lee and his cronies and Gina in a social situation; Lee hosting a party, and James; Lee and alcohol and drugs and his cronies; and Gina . . . almost as soon as he mentions it. It was a Monday, I remember.

He came to therapy at half past six. He was in ebullient mood. He was going to Cornwall that weekend with Gina, he loved Cornwall. He'd found out it was her birthday on Thursday and suggested they do something nice; take the day off, there was an exhibition that she wanted to see. He was going to drive her down on Friday, that meant only two more days of work to go. He was feeling good. He was going to have some people round, yeah, maybe have a dinner. A big one. He could have it in the garden – it's summer. He could have it Thursday night before he went to Cornwall. No, that was Gina's birthday, Wednesday then, he had the next day off. She could have some people too. A kind of birthday party. You know, he hasn't had anyone round since before the accident. Before then, everyone used to congregate at his – on a Friday prior to going out, in the early hours coming back; he didn't do that any more, he hadn't realized, it must have been a confidence thing.

If only I'd said, 'I advise you not to do that yet, you're not yet ready,' because I'd had a premonition – alcohol, drugs, Gina, James, Lee with his weakness; if only I'd said.

But maybe today will be the end of his haunting of me, the end of my nightmares. Blame will be apportioned, and not just for his death; for his life. He was easily led, I always thought, but that wasn't true, I couldn't lead him. He let James do that, all the way through, even after his eyes had been opened, let himself down, let Gina—

Everything happened because of the party he threw for her birthday, he *apparently* threw for her birthday, everything happened because of that night.

Four

I pull the cord which stops the bus. Last time. I disembark. Walk the little stretch along this road I've walked for all these weeks. Never again. Up these steps. Courtroom number five. Never another morning like this.

In the corridor outside, milling around or lining the walls on benches, the cast of this drama. Bob smoking a surreptitious cigarette, Nancy chewing her nails; Gina arriving with James's mother, joining his father pacing up and down; Cabresi, not chatting, with Lizzie; Lara with her honey blonde hair; Joseph . . .

Joseph?

He comes over to me, I say, 'What are you doing here?'

'I came to see if you were okay?'

'Me?'

'Yes. Today's the day, isn't it?'

'Yes.'

'I thought you might want a friendly face.'

'Thank you,' I say, pleased and perplexed, unsettled a little.

We take our places. In the public gallery we have arranged ourselves left and right. Gina sits on the left. James enters, flanked by policemen, shown to the dock. The balding pate, the lack in the chin, how could she kiss him? When she touched him did she think of Lee? His unexpected softness.

All rise. The judge comes in, the lawyers poise to strike, the jury bides its time. Has it made up its mind, does it already know? We sit.

But what will I do once it's over?

Five

Such luxury the past few weeks have been, hearing it all told back to me. This narrative, which had been playing in my head for so many months, now plays externally. But only for one more day. This life which I found so intriguing, this death which embroiled me, that night in the Orange Room with which the Prosecution begins summing up:

'"You've gone too far this time," Lee said to James. He threatened him, "You're over." Two days later Lee was dead.'

There's a plethora of circumstantial evidence, there's a witness to place James at the scene, there's a motive – but you can never tell with justice. What will the jury decide? Gina was living with him when it happened, but she'd left his house at six o'clock that night to go to work, so he doesn't have an alibi. Gina was living with him when it happened, Gina was with James.

He was her lover like Lee never was, like he should have been, like he would have been if only he'd gone to Cornwall with Gina, if James hadn't messed it up.

Six

I'd like to tell Lee I've seen Gina. I'd like to give him a progress report on the whole situation. The way James just sits there, the look in his eyes, the doubt on her face, I can't tell him. I tell him anyway. It wasn't so different when he was alive. The myriad things I wished I could tell him. Therapy's only one side of the story. This is my side.

Seven

Lee said, 'I've started over once, I don't think I can do it again.' I agreed with him. Now, I go over and over it, hoping the end might change. Even in this courtroom, listening to the Prosecution, I keep wishing it's not going to happen the way that I know it will. How far would I have to go back to alter the outcome? To that day I agreed with him? To the party he gave? To Gina's arrival? To me? To falling in love with Lizzie? To meeting James? To Cabresi? To Bob and Nancy? If he'd done, if she'd done, but most of all if I'd done; I almost believe if I keep going over it, things might end differently.

Or else, things might make sense. I might see it all clearly. Cause and effect. No other way for events to turn out. Peace then.

Eight

But the only thing retrospect gives me is the knowledge of how it was able to happen, not why, it doesn't rub out regret, doesn't give reason. I need reason like some cosmic force, some master plan; it had to happen like this because ... I need meaning. Some people believe that nothing's coincidence, that every relationship's karmic, I wish that I did. I wish I believed that all of this was preordained. I don't want to think that life is all there is and Lee is dead.

Nine

It's the second time that James has been in court for him. What are the chances of that? He found Lee a lawyer I remember, paid the fees; why, I wonder, guilty conscience? I wonder if the lawyer's the same? He's clever, deadpan, waves evidence away as though it were nothing serious, dismisses the Prosecution's motive as preposterous. He got Lee acquitted. Will he do the same for James?

The terror I felt, taking the stand, reminding myself I was merely a witness, merely recalling that night in the club with Joseph, just as he had recalled it no need for nerves. But the faces . . . Bob, Nancy, Cabresi . . . The eyes on me . . . Watching intently, wanting to know . . . That lawyer against me. Wondering if the heat and discomfort I feel on the inside show on the outside. He makes me feel guilty.

'On the 4th of September last year,' he said, 'you were having a drink in the Orange Room.'

'Yes.'

'Were you acquainted with the Accused before that night?'

'I had met him once before.'

'And where was that?'

'In the Orange Room.'

'In the Orange Room, at the bar.'

'Yes.'

'You were the Deceased's psychoanalyst.'

'Yes.'

'Do you mix with your clients socially?'

'No.'

'But you were in the Orange Room on the night in question?'

'Yes. I've been a member of that club for over ten years.'

'A club which the Deceased used to frequent.'

'Yes.'

'He told you this?'

'He mentioned it.'

'Had you ever seen him there before?'

'No. I don't go often.'

'But you had seen the Accused.'

'Yes, once.'

'Once.'

'Yes. About four weeks earlier.'

'You said you don't go often.'

'No.'

'But enough to meet the Accused and then to meet him again four weeks later?'

'Yes.'

'And on both occasions you struck up a conversation?'

'Yes.'

'Not knowing that this man was the best friend whom your client had talked of – often – in his therapy sessions?'

'No.'

'You had no idea.'

'No.'

'He told you his name was James?'

'Yes.'

'But you didn't think he might be the Deceased's friend, James?'

'I didn't put the two together.'

'He was the right age, he was in the right bar—?'

'It never occurred to me.'

'Never?'

'No. Lee wasn't in my thoughts. I wasn't working.'

'You just happened, coincidentally, to get into a long conversation with your client's best friend.'

'Yes.'

'Do you often talk to strangers in bars, Mr Locke?'

'No.'

'And yet you talked to this stranger.'

'Yes.'

'This stranger who, *coincidentally*, you actually knew a good deal about.'

'Yes.'

'Yes. I'm just finding the coincidence hard to believe. Why did you talk to him, Mr Locke?'

'I fancied him,' I said, and my whole stomach turned over at the thought.

'You found him attractive and you started to talk with him?'

'Yes.'

'What did you talk about?'

'Mainly about the fact that I didn't like the place we were in.'

'You don't like the Orange Room?'

'I find it pretentious.'

'And yet you went there a few weeks later.'

'Yes.'

'Can you tell me why that was?'

'I was with a friend. We'd had dinner. We talked about the club, he said he'd never been there before. I said I was a member and he asked me to take him.'

'And you saw the Accused at the bar.'

'Yes.'

'And you spoke to him.'

'He spoke to me.'

'What did he say?'

'He said, "I thought you hated this place," or something like that.'

Ten

Joseph's hand on my arm brings me back to the present. I look down. Such long fingers. Everyone's standing, I realize. All rise.

There should be something more than this as the jury departs to make its decision, as we troop outside for the wait. A cello concerto in a minor key, something grandiose, sweeping, significant. There should be something—

When I'm at home I listen to music, the view from my windows an oddly appropriate backdrop. This car replacing that car in a steady stream, like notes; the humdrum of the street – leaving here, coming back, passing in-between, buses caught, roads crossed – the music gives it meaning. Almost breathed, sighed out. Funny sometimes. Sometimes faintly tragic. Lee gave me music.

Discovering it was falling in love, going to hear it was going on dates, the dressing up, the nervous excitement, something to look forward to, the world seeming right. It didn't have much to do with Lee after a while. He was the catalyst, the door handle. Now it wasn't just cellists, it was piano sonatas, it was choral works, it wasn't just classical music, it was jazz, it was African drummers, it was Brazilian guitarists. After a while it was Joseph.

Last summer the church in the square where I work started putting on concerts. Lunchtime recitals by students – Joseph was one of them. We met on the steps of the church, him smoking a cigarette, me enjoying the sunshine. He said, 'I see you here every day.' He was young enough to be enthused by my enthusiasm, professional enough to find it endearing. I said, 'Isn't that bad for your playing?' He laughed and threw the cigarette away.

We went to a concert together the following week, and another the week after that. Perhaps he was glad of somebody to buy the tickets. I was glad to have another particular interest in being there, an interest that had nothing to do with Lee. It made me feel involved, accompanying a real musician, not an imaginary one, and one who had his career ahead of him. I didn't envisage they'd meet.

But would we be friends without that night in the Orange Room, statements to make, this court case to bind us? Would we be friends still? Friends like I wasn't with Lee. Lee gave me Joseph.

Eleven

Not much noise in the lobby of this courtroom. Rustle of bodies, footsteps approaching and dying away. Nobody talking. Everyone concentrating. Not much to do. Trip to the bathroom, trip to the coffee dispenser, trip outside with Joseph to watch him smoke a cigarette. Guilty verdict. It must be guilty.

Lizzie and Michael Cabresi sit next to each other, not moving. I imagine what it's like to be them in this moment. This present trauma made all the harder because it comes from the past, so many years without him in between. The scar on her face more vivid in this light than it was in the courtroom, but still not so bad, not as bad as he described it, from her left eye, down her cheek, to her mouth.

The months it took for him to describe it, to tell me what happened, I knew all about it, I had it in my notes. The wreck that he was when I met him, eyes cast downwards, fingers jutting out. The result of a fracas, the reason he's here, it doesn't get a mention. I wait for him. I wait. And finally, they start to come out, the details of that evening.

Twelve

It was a Friday night like any other. He and James went to a pub in the centre of town. He hadn't been having it easy lately, he couldn't get work, things were over with Lizzie, this was to cheer him up. James was buying the drinks, he'd got a couple of wraps; he gave one to Lee.

The bar was crowded, nowhere to sit, pretty much nowhere to stand. It made him feel better already, the sound of everyone's voices, drinks in glasses, it gave him a buzz. And Lara turned up. He hadn't seen her for ages. He was so pleased to see her. He hugged her. He said, 'What are you doing here?'

It was just what he needed, just who he needed to see. His spirits had taken a bashing since leaving the orchestra, since splitting from Lizzie, she and Cabresi were family, his world had been pulled from under his feet. He felt sixteen again, the same terrible low of leaving home, terrible fear, an abyss underneath him; but this time there wasn't a patron, this time he was really alone.

Not tonight in this bar, all these people, something about

it felt permanent; James, his friend then, his friend now, and Lara. Lara laughing at him like he was funny, smiling at him like he was handsome – there'd always been that spark between them – perhaps she felt like it tonight.

For a while he didn't see Lizzie. He was stopped when he did, but then he smiled and waved. She didn't wave back. A shot of fury went through him, then passed – she was the one who'd hurt him, she didn't even deserve his greeting; then it passed: he was on form, having fun, nothing could touch him. He didn't notice her come over until she was standing in front of him. He said, 'Hello.'

'Hi!' said Lara.

Lizzie didn't say anything.

That anger again, hot, what did she think she was doing? Ruining his life. Spoiling his evening.

'Get me a beer,' said Lara.

'Sure,' said Lee.

'And one for her.'

He turned around to order.

There was a silence behind him, then Lara prattling on, he couldn't hear what she was saying. All the time he was waiting, all the time ordering, his back turned, he could feel Lizzie's speechless presence, could see her as though he faced the other way, could hear the thoughts racing through her mind. He gave Lizzie a drink. He gave Lara hers. Lara kissed him.

Lara kissed him full on the lips like she did it for effect and he kissed her back, it seemed a sort of revenge. But while he was doing this (it must have been then, though he hadn't been looking) Lizzie broke her bottle against the wall of the bar; Lara pulled away from him and turned around, Lizzie swung it upwards—

It would have got Lara's face if he hadn't caught it. He caught it in his left hand, its jagged edge slicing his fingers. The sudden pain of it, the pain and the reflex action. It was just a reflex action. He brought it down on Lizzie's head, smashing the unbroken end that she had been holding, cutting her forehead, cutting her eye, cutting her cheek . . .

He said there was a silence then. Time stood still. He looked round at Lara whose eyes were wide. He looked at James looking back. He looked down at Lizzie who had fallen to the floor . . . Noise suddenly resumed again.

Thirteen

Thinking about him telling me the story, telling it to me falteringly, the more he trusts me the more information leaking out, thinking about the way he trusts, that amazing vulnerability. He always thought it coincidence that Lizzie and Lara were both there that evening, I had my doubts. It didn't surprise me when I heard Lizzie's testimony, heard her say that she'd bumped into James earlier that day, that he'd told her their plans. Did he do it on purpose? Did anyone else notice? Did he invite Lara as well? Six years later he'd bring her to Gina's birthday party; that night would herald another major decline. Before, it was Lee's career which ended, now everything would end, everything, James would take it all away, please God, today the wait is over. We are called.

Fourteen

These moments are the very worst, these moments bind us all in one experience no matter what our bias, despite which result we're hoping to hear. Vague coldness, vague sickness, everything-depends-on-this, no hope, no despair. James is led to the dock.

I can't take my eyes from him. I watch him smile at Gina, her smile back, watch the man asking the question – 'Have you reached a verdict on which you are all agreed?' – watch James's parents, his sisters, him, something so much bigger than them, '. . . Do you find the Defendant James Christopher Benson . . .' nobody breathing—

'Guilty.'

Joseph patting my hand.

Bob and Nancy embracing each other, Cabresi and Lizzie, Gina closing her eyes. Gina. What is it like to be her in this moment? 'James Christopher Benson,' the judge is saying; what does she think, that her lover wasn't capable of it? If he didn't do it, who else did? No expression on his face as he hears his fate, imprisonment for life, no less than fifteen years; a shrug, a shake of the head, this helplessness, utter, unbargained-for, but inured to it now.

Fifteen

'You must be pleased,' says Joseph.

'I feel numb,' I reply.

He looks at me pointlessly. Everyone's leaving, everyone's

walking away, Cabresi, Lizzie, Bob and Nancy walking down these steps, Lara, Gina, everything ended, everyone gone.

I say, 'I feel like he's died all over again.'

'What now, then?' says Joseph.

He means it more immediately, but it's the question that's been scaring me. This verdict was my goal, was Lee's, we've got it, who knows how life continues after that?

'I'm just going to go home.'

'Will you be okay?'

'I'll be fine.'

'Do you want some company?'

'No. No, you're sweet.' I put my hand to his shoulder. Mainly to stop him from hugging me, he's a very physical person, Joseph. Tactile. I walk away.

I hail a cab. Don't want to be thinking, on the bus ride home from the courtroom, never make this journey again. Never occupy my day like this. Another step away from him.

It shouldn't be sunny, the sun shining onto my face through the windows of this taxi, making everything look happy. First days of summer, all of it hopeful, all of it new. There will never be anything worse than this feeling. Never be regret like this ever again. Never this kind of mourning. This reproach for the effect that he had, the way I reacted. It was a madness. Looking back on it now I see it as a madness and I wish it were possible to play it all again. In my present state, how differently I would behave, how much more objective I'd be able to be. But we get sucked in, all of us. We are all no further than a kiss from chaos.

I close my eyes. The sun's on my eyelids. Reminds me

what it's like for a moment to be living in the present. The utter importance of it, the up and down like a love affair, as if I had everything vested in the way it turned out. It could have turned out perfectly. It seemed so likely towards the end of his life. He wasn't drinking much, wasn't taking drugs, he was giving all that a rest for a while, he wanted to get his head straight. He was feeling pretty calm, but there'd been a period before Gina moved in when he'd lurched from one extreme to another, it was exhausting, he wanted to empty out, know who he was, no external stimulus. I watched him, I knew that feeling.

So proud, so proud suddenly. Perhaps it was just about connections, perhaps that was all it was. Just wanted us to have had a similar experience, something on a level, something understood. I shouldn't have done it. I began actively to involve myself, fill his head with my ideas, egg him on. He was so susceptible. He wanted change.

But it all came at once for him, too much at once, transforming his life, falling for Gina, falling out with James. I should have let the latter happen slowly. I was impatient. I asked pointed questions, stirred the pot. Stirred him up so he wasn't certain what was true and what was not, what the fuck he was doing. Thinking, thinking, trying to work it out. Everything he'd told me, now told with a different slant, his whole past changed. James was never a friend. Wanting excuse for the way he'd let this man in, let himself be controlled, wanting reason.

James sniffed it on the air, read Lee's changing mind, he started to panic, called him three times a day, sometimes with nothing to say, and Lee, infested by me, began to look for subtext. 'He's worried,' he told me. 'He can't stand it that I'm getting a life.' Infested by me. But we were right.

Some friend of a friend of James's had bought a place. It used to be seventeen bedsits, he wanted to convert it into a three-storey house with a flat in the basement. Lee got the job. The money from that would really get him started, was something he could get really into, a real project with real input. He was happy, living in the home he'd made, falling in love with Gina. He *was* getting a life. James couldn't stand it.

Sixteen

I pay the driver. I think, James took it all away. I walk to my block, ride to my floor, home. But Lee helped him, it hurt me, Lee was so predictable. I open all the windows. Perhaps people behave in the way we expect them to behave, perhaps that's all we see, perhaps they have no choice. It seemed so positive then, but I knew he'd let me down, knew it was nothing but the high before the low. I remember the day he came to see me, a month before he died, he was in ebullient mood, he was going to Cornwall that weekend with Gina . . . I remember I stopped listening. Started imagining, without control, without awareness (until something he said brought me back again) what the weekend would hold, whether it would finally happen, consummation, he hadn't made love since the accident.

'It's her birthday on Thursday,' he told me, 'I thought I might get some people round.'

'Will you invite James?'

'I've got to,' he said.

But almost as soon as he mentioned it I foresaw disaster ahead.

The party was on Wednesday night; Thursday I expected him at six o'clock. In bed the night before I tried to imagine how our meeting would go. Not well. No matter how I thought, rethought, rewound, the scene would always dissolve into nastiness, this nastiness would always come sooner and sooner until it was the very point when he came through my door. How much of it, then, was my responsibility? Next day, at six o'clock, he crashed in. He was drunk. His jaw was set in a cocaine fury. The evening, he told me, had been a disaster, throwing out the sentence like some challenge, like an accusation. I said nothing. 'It totally went off,' he sneered at me. I kept silent. 'I got fucking off my head,' he said; I didn't say anything. For a while, in this manner, we fought each other. Then he said, 'I can't handle this,' and left.

Seventeen

Everything happened because of that night, Lee's behaviour that night. My disappointment was real, as my hopes had been fantasy ... But it wasn't his fault really, it wasn't wholly his. It was James. James brought the two things that he knew would shake Lee up, he brought Lara and he brought cocaine, and then he left. The next morning Gina called round to see him. She didn't know what to do, Lee was off his head, he'd been up all night, he was like a different person; James told her to go back. He made her some tea, rolled her a joint, just time enough, told her to go back there, knew what she'd find.

Eighteen

'I was nervous,' he says to me, 'Nervous like you wouldn't believe. I wanted everything to be perfect for Gina. I wanted everything to be perfect for me. I hadn't had anyone round for years.

'I didn't know what to make. I thought I'd do a barbecue. I hoped it wouldn't rain, hoped everything would cook, didn't know what to buy, took the afternoon off to go to the shops, got everything ready.

'Then Gina was late. She'd said she'd be there to give me a hand, but she wasn't. I was on my own when people started arriving. Then James turned up with Lara.

'I couldn't believe it. I hadn't seen her since that business with Lizzie. It brought it all back. The fear, the need to justify myself, I didn't have any idea what she thought of me. She was nice to me, though. I was relieved. In an anxious kind of way. Kind of grateful.

'There were about ten of us, all in the garden, all on the furniture I'd made, eating from the barbecue I'd made, in the house I'd made. It felt good. But I was vulnerable, too. Lara sat next to me. Gina down the other end.

'Afterwards, everyone sitting round that table said they could see it was going to go off but I didn't notice. I honestly didn't. I was too busy keeping everything together, my head together, filling up glasses and plates. It was Wednesday so people started to leave about midnight. By one, it was just me, Gina, James and Lara. Then Lara says she wants some coke.

'I didn't have any so James called Tony. I thought he'd just pop in and everyone would do a line and that would be it. But he came round with his girlfriend and about four wraps. James left.

'Lara said, "Are you two still in each other's pockets?"

'"No," I said, "it's kind of cooled off." She did an impersonation of his father which made us laugh.

'Gina said, "He's such a freak. He's always telling me to be careful of Lee. Last week he said I only knew seventy per cent of him, then he said Lee could make a girl go mad. This morning he said I should have seen what happened to his last girlfriend . . ."

'No one said anything for ages. "You know, I'm not sure I needed to hear that," I said.

'When the coke came out again she went to bed. I should have gone with her. I should have left it at that, chucked everyone out. But the whole day had been such a roller coaster. And you know what I'm like with cocaine . . . I was just starting to relax.'

Nineteen

The world carries on outside my windows. Still light, the long summer evenings just beginning. Not even a year ago. A night like tonight. At the time it sounded like excuses, but I see now, I appreciate his state of mind. In my present calm how differently I would react, how much more objective I'd be able to be. Then, though, I had an agenda.

I'd been through it with Lee, I'd broken my heart for him, the interest I'd taken, the hope; then James, then the girls, then drugs ... I'd taken him out of my head.

But one Monday he came to see me, a new expression on his face. Suddenly a thought went through me – Gina and Lee – one thought and I was in again.

But it all came at once, his decision to stop going out so much, his deepening involvement with Gina, his footing with James slipping away. He was picking apart the most enduring, important relationship of his life and finding nothing at its core. It was too much at once, I see that now; then, though, I had an agenda. Gina and Lee. Gina ousting James. Gina was my hope. When he slighted her, he slighted me.

Twenty

How silly it all seems now in the quiet of my flat, in light of his death, the passage of time in between. I thought when he died, At least it might give a kind of relief, the struggle will be gone. But now I empathize, now I feel guilt, I was impatient with him, inconsiderate of how hard it had been, I only saw my own expectations not being met, I never cut him any slack ...

How much slack, though, did he ever cut anybody?

I was lucky in a way because I was able to hear Gina's side of the story, see her taking the stand; suddenly, then, the whole thing became real. Before, it had seemed like a fantasy, my fantasy, it felt like a terrible responsibility. I steered him towards it, I slighted James, I paid more attention when he talked about Gina, I thought his friendship with James would fail because of her, I thought it.

But I never imagined this end. Gina and James together, Lee dead.

It was her birthday, she said, she was taking Lee to Cornwall. They'd been sharing a bed for the past few weeks, since the roof started leaking. He hadn't touched her. He had but he hadn't, in a way that made her want him all the more. She was different. Not like the girls he used to sleep with, that she could hear him having sex with from her room next door, that she'd be jealous of if there hadn't been so many.

Maybe she'd misread the signs. She thought that he loved her. Maybe he didn't fancy her. But they started spending so much time together, he started kissing the back of her neck in bed, he was holding a party so she'd meet his friends, they were going away that weekend, it was going to happen.

She felt threatened by Lara. Lara was older, more confident, Lara had Lee round her finger. He was jumpy, eager to please, he sat down next to her, the only place for Gina right down the other end.

When everyone else left, she wouldn't go. She wanted some drugs. James made a phone call and Tony turned up with his girlfriend Sam. James went.

As soon as he'd gone Lara and Lee started laughing about him like he was a joke that they shared, and they alone, so Gina joined in. She was asserting her claim with the comment she made but she didn't realize till later, till James filled her in about Lizzie (how could he have done it?) why it made Lee go funny and immediately do another line. She wanted to talk to him. She wanted to be alone with him. She went to bed because she thought it would break up the party. It was two in the morning, she thought Lee would follow. It was her birthday tomorrow, he was taking her to an exhibition and then out to dinner after therapy, and then down to Cornwall on Friday, he couldn't afford to stay up and get trashed.

She got into bed and heard him go to the bathroom. She hoped he'd come in before he went back downstairs. He did. He peeked round the side of the door and caught sight of her grinning at him from his pillow. He hugged her. She cuddled him back. He said, 'I did tonight all for you and everyone loved you.'

'I loved tonight.'

'You were the belle of the ball.'

She kissed his lips. They kissed each other's lips a couple of times. He said, 'I'm going to get high now,' and grimaced at her. 'You don't mind, do you?'

'No.'

'We've got all weekend.'

'Get as high as you like.' He kissed her again and went back downstairs.

She fell asleep. She woke an hour or so later when Lee lay down beside her, he put one arm underneath her and the other around her, he pulled her in. He said, 'Am I in trouble?'

'No.'

He got up. He said, 'I've come to get some jumpers. The kids are getting cold.' He grabbed some sweatshirts out of a drawer. He said, 'I'm being such a good host.'

She got up too and put her arms around him. She said, 'When are you coming to bed?'

'Ten minutes.'

'I like cuddling up to you,' she said

'I like cuddling up to you too,' he said, lifting her up, putting her back into bed.

When she woke it was light; she had heard the door close. She looked at the clock, 5.30, and thought everyone had left. She went downstairs. But actually, Sam and Lara had just gone to the garage for cigarettes. They came back and started dancing to Stevie Wonder in the sitting room. Gina tried to dance too but she couldn't, she was in her dressing gown, she felt sober. Lee was on the table, Lara gyrating in front of him. He wasn't noticing, but it still made Gina feel weird. She couldn't get into their rhythm, she was straight and they were not. It was so confusing. Everything seemed to make no sense, not humour, not words, not mood. Tony cut up four lines on the mirror. Sam said, 'Quiz?' and Lee embraced her. 'We love Sam,' he said.

If she went to sleep, she thought, she'd wake up and it would be over, everyone gone, things back to normal, Lee lying beside her, happy birthday, Gina . . . She got into bed but she couldn't drift off. After a while she got dressed. They were all in the garden, Lee looking ugly, who knows how much coke he'd been snorting, he was shouting angrily at Lara, 'Why do you want to be men?'

'Don't be ridiculous.'

'What *do* you want, then? What do *you* want, Gina?'

'Sorry?'

'It's coming back on you because we don't want you. Men don't want women like you.'

She went upstairs, she took off her clothes, she got back into bed.

She lay there. For hours it seemed like, unable to sleep because of the music, because of the noise from downstairs, the thought of the whole situation, how anxious it made her, nothing to do. Nothing? She wrapped herself up in Lee's duvet and went back down to cause a scene. 'Look at the eyes on her,' said Tony.

'I can't believe you're still here.'

'It's a party,' said Lee.

'Haven't you got jobs to go to?'

'She's got a face on her,' said Tony.

'She knows it too,' said Lee.

'Jesus,' she said, and lay down on the grass.

'Gina! That's my white duvet cover.'

'I don't care, I can't sleep upstairs, the music's too loud.'

'It's your fault,' said Sam, 'cos you're the host and you're not telling us to leave.'

'We should call you Caspar,' said Tony, 'you look just like Caspar the Ghost.'

'I like that,' said Lee, 'it suits her. Hey, Caspar, are you having a horrible time?'

'Yes I am.'

'Line anyone?' said Tony, and went into the kitchen.

'I'm really over it, Lee,' she said as he made to follow him.

'Well I'm not.'

'It's 7.30 in the morning.'

'Who cares what time it is?'

'I do.'

He sighed. He said, 'I hardly ever have a blow-out like this, Gina, I hardly ever have the day off . . . I need this. To get out my aggression.' Lara went into the kitchen. 'And she's here,' said Lee, 'and I haven't seen her for ages.'

Gina ran a bath, trying to kill time. She stayed in it for as long as she could, got into bed, tried to sleep, couldn't, noticed it was 9.15, angrily got dressed again, went back downstairs. She said, 'Lee – I'm going out.'

'Oh, don't go,' said Lara, 'I'm about to make cocktails.'

'Where are you going?' asked Lee.

'I don't know.'

'Well . . . It'd be really nice if you came back.'

'You what?'

'It'd be really nice—'

'I'll see you,' she said, and she left.

But after she left she didn't really know what to do. She had expected Lee to say, 'Don't go, you're right, this has gone on long enough,' but he hadn't, and she'd come downstairs without a jacket on, with no money on her, only carrying her front-door keys. She walked down the road a little way and sat on the bench at the end of the block. She wondered what to do. How long could she sit there? How long would she have to sit there before going back home? How long till they left? Would they leave? That hideous Lara. That horrible side of Lee. She saw James on the other side of the street, walking home, carrying milk, she ran over to him. 'What's the matter?' he said.

Twenty-one

As if he didn't know. As if he hadn't known what Lee would do with Lara there, with all that coke. He took Gina back to his flat. He said, 'What's happened?' and she told him about it, Lee up all night, with those people, the amount of cocaine, Lara being territorial, Lee playing her game, making Gina feel like a party pooper, it was her party supposedly, her birthday, her weekend with Lee; she'd been so looking forward to it, it should have started yesterday, right now she should be waking up with Lee, instead she felt like going to Cornwall without him.

'Don't do that,' said James.

'Leave it a while,' he said, 'they can't stay forever, it's nearly ten. Have some tea, smoke a joint; calm down. Then ring him and check that they've gone and go back. Have your weekend. Sort it out later.'

'You warned me about him.'

'It'll be fine.'

'You think?'

'Yes,' he said, 'go back in a minute.' As if he didn't know what she'd find.

She let herself in. The house was quiet. She went upstairs and into Lee's room. He didn't wake up. Lara did. She opened her eyes. She smiled.

She was lying on her back in her bra and pants, Lee curled

naked around her. Like he usually was with Gina, in the bed that she'd just got out of, his grass-stained duvet in a heap on the floor. Lara prodded him and he opened his eyes.

'Sorry,' said Gina, 'I did try to ring but there was no answer.'

'I was probably asleep,' said Lee.

'Right. Are you still coming to Cornwall?'

'It's Thursday,' he snapped. And then, a little more gently, 'We should talk downstairs.'

He pulled a sarong from the back of the door and tied it round his waist then walked out of the room. Gina followed him.

'I'm not married to you, you know,' he said as he went down the stairs.

'I know.'

'What did you think you were doing? Coming down in my duvet, having a strop, storming out?'

'That,' she said, pointing to the ceiling where Lara lay in bed above it, 'was on the cards all evening. How would you like it if I invited my friends round here and ended up in bed with one of them?'

'To be honest,' he said, 'it wouldn't really bother me.'

'No,' she said, 'I bet it wouldn't. Happy birthday, Gina.

'It's rude apart from anything else,' she said. 'We had plans today. I took time off work.'

He said, 'You don't live in the modern world.'

'It's sleazy.'

'Don't judge me.'

'The sad thing is,' she said, 'James was right.'

'I put on last night all for you.'

'Yeah and it was lovely, and then drugs arrived and I just went out the window.'

'You're right,' said Lee, his mood suddenly changing, 'I think we should talk about that.'

'No,' said Gina, 'let's not. Let's just go out and go away and have a nice time . . .'

'No,' he said, 'I need to hear it. And I'm sure you've got a lot to say about it. Just give me ten minutes to get dressed.'

He left the room, Gina sat on the sofa. She looked in the mirror. She looked a wreck. She went to the bathroom and started putting her make-up on, and while she was doing this she started to feel really uncomfortable, really manic. She couldn't give him ten minutes. She couldn't give him one minute longer. She knew she was going to blow things up but she couldn't help herself. She left the bathroom and went to his bedroom, quickly before she could change her mind. Lara was lying across the bed. Lee was crouching over her, his bottom making figures of eight in the air. It froze when he heard her.

Twenty-two

He barged into my room at six that evening. He was drunk. His nose was red and starting to crack as though he had a cold. The dinner, he told me, had been a disaster. 'It totally went off,' he sneered at me, 'I got fucking off my head . . . Gina found me in bed with Lara—'

I couldn't speak because I didn't know what I'd say. I waited for him to do the talking, to tell me one of those horrific stories that used to work me up, but he didn't. He stayed silent. Eventually he said, 'I can't handle this,' and left.

Twenty-three

I feel anxious, I realize, anxious just recalling the event, a fraction of the way I felt that day, winded, a heavy emptiness inside; I pour myself a glass of wine to calm me down.

I remember, I caught myself flitting from one task to another, pacing, unable to keep my thoughts together. The disappointment was real, all my hopes had been ridiculous dreams. It lurked in the back of my mind, in the pit of my stomach. The following day he turned up at my office. I was busy with clients, but he waited. He waited three hours. Finally, he asked if he could take me to lunch.

Funny, then, to be walking down the road with him, in public with him, it didn't give the feeling I'd imagined. Perhaps that was circumstantial. He looked awful. Too old, I thought, to be drinking all night, his skin couldn't take it . . . We went to a place round the corner.

He said, 'I feel like shit. I've lost out on a really nice weekend, I've probably lost a very good friend, and it's all my fault.' He said, 'Yesterday, after I saw you, I went home and called James. I *knew* Gina was round there. I just had a feeling. He didn't pick up. I went over this morning. No one was there. I called her mobile. I got voicemail.'

I said, 'What do you want me to say to you?'

'Do you think she'll give me another chance? Should I call her again?'

'If you want to.'

That evening he rang me at home. He said, 'I've left several messages for Gina. The last one said, "I know you don't want to speak to me and I totally understand, but I would like to give my side of the story." I've had no response.'

'Lee, this isn't really my remit.'

'I can't believe that I've done this.'

'We can talk when you come in on Monday.'

But he wouldn't stop talking. How awful he felt, how stupid he'd been, he'd really fucked up, he'd never meant to hurt her, maudlin self-pity. I listened to him. Sitting on that chair, on that telephone, his voice on the other end, his voice that three weeks later I'd never hear again, I heard only my own disappointment. It lurked in the back of my mind, in the pit of my stomach. I confronted it, talked myself round. I was stupid ever to imagine that he'd sort himself out, I told myself, but I know it now, at least I know it now. It gave a kind of comfort. He rang me twice that night. He rang me to pour out his guilt and then he rang to say he'd called James on his mobile. James was in Cornwall with Gina.

Twenty-four

It didn't occur to him that this was a problem. He didn't imagine that Gina would be doing anything other than breaking her heart for him. I expected him at least to have spent the weekend, as I had, thinking the worst, but on Monday he turned up to our session completely believing things would be fine. It was amazing to me, the speed with which he moved on from disaster. Something had happened, he'd been wracked with self-loathing and guilt, then he'd come to a conclusion about the way he'd behaved, and why, and it was as if this conclusion obliterated the act itself. *Oh, that's all right then.* He walked in looking confident, wearing a blue checked shirt. He'd shaved. He said, 'I've been getting my head straight all weekend.

'The thing is,' he said, 'the body of a cello is like the body of a woman – all curves. That's why I'm so resentful of them.' He scanned my face for a reaction to this verdict. 'I want to hurt them,' he said, 'especially the ones I like, because subconsciously ... It's to do with lack of choice. I never wanted to be a musician,' he emphasized. '*It* chose *me.*'

'Did you see Gina last night?' I asked him.

'She hasn't got back yet. I'll see her later. I'll explain. The other evening,' he said, 'I blame it on Lara. I haven't worked out what her motives were yet ... But there are various things I've learnt, and one is, be very careful who you invite to a party. Another one is, end the party at eleven – or better still! Have it at lunchtime. I was speaking to Tony,' he said, 'about that night, and he said, in London you fall out with, on average, a thousand people a year.'

'You think you meet a thousand people a year?'

'And you know what else? Sex is all about proximity.'

Twenty-five

But when he got home after therapy Gina's things were gone. He told me he thought she was over-reacting. Maybe she was.

Maybe she was and maybe I was too but that barbecue had started a chain reaction, a domino effect, a switch had flicked in my head. Nothing he did after that could be right. Nothing I thought about him could be positive. It was like falling out of love, nothing worse than that, finding the object of your passion unworthy. All good things, then, seem an illusion.

Even the cello, I remember thinking, something so majestic and yet ultimately pathetic about it, it almost whinges. How very appropriate. He was one of those patients who enters therapy insisting they want to change when all they want to do is stay the same while the therapist makes them feel better. 'I've never met anyone as introspective as you,' I told him in one of our few subsequent sessions, but I could see he was taking it as a compliment. He behaved like his life was a film. In films, people applaud the rascal. But in reality they tire of them quickly, and either destroy them, or sit back and watch them destroy themselves. I felt tired of him. Not that this didn't hurt me.

That amazing anger he had within him, that glint I saw in his eye almost as soon as I met him, it frightened me and drew me in; that anger (which could also express itself as passion) for friends, music, life. But the thing which repels you attracts you, only finally to repel you. By Thursday he was angry. Gina hadn't returned. He told me he thought she was staying with James. He wondered if James was stirring things up but he couldn't be bothered to go round and find out – he'd tried to make it up with her several times, if this was how she wanted to behave, then fine.

She was passive-aggressive. She was manipulative. Just as Cabresi was, just as James was, just as Lara was, he was just a puppet in everyone else's game, everyone had an agenda.

'And me?'

'You don't count. You don't care.'

'That's what you think?'

'I pay you.'

'That's what you say is it? To your friends? "Peter doesn't care."'

'I'd never say "Peter".'

'Sorry?'

'I'd never say your name. No one knows your name. You're "that man I go to see" or something. I like it better like that.'

Twenty-six

That weekend he saw James and Gina out together. It made his heart beat. It made his heart beat in his head. His mouth went dry and his pupils dilated, he was sensitive to the way his adrenaline rushed, he felt rooted to the spot, he felt hot all over, frightened and furious. Gina seemed to have got over it fine. She was laughing and joking, letting James whisper in her ear, letting herself find it hysterical. He would have thought she was doing it on purpose but she seemed not to have noticed him. But women could do that, couldn't they, see out of the corners of their eyes. There were just a few things he wanted to say, a few things he'd like to explain. He went over. He said, 'Gina—'

She turned away.

'For God's sake . . . All I want to do is talk to you. You want a scene?'

'That's enough,' said James.

'What's it got to do with you? What is it with you anyway? Is this down to you?'

He must have told her about Lizzie. God knows what he said about Lizzie. He must have told the bedsit guy too, because when Lee rang him on Monday about starting the job, the whole thing was off.

Twenty-seven

Everything I'd disregarded now became clear, every dispensation now went. His studies, his career, his relationship with Lizzie, Gina, every chance he's ever had, ruined . . . because of his childhood, the trauma of college, his early promotion, the accident – it's reason, but it isn't excuse.

And anyway, there are reasons for everything, it's only now I've learned to look beyond them. Or rather, in front of them, at the creature which presents itself and not to delve around. He might behave in a certain way and I might understand, I might even forgive, but never the less I hurt. Reasons are irrelevant.

He's self-destructive, he's generally destructive . . . Look what happened to Lizzie – because of the stress he was under finding a job, because of his broken heart, because of events beyond his control, the state of his mind, but look what happened to Lizzie. I wasn't there, I only heard it the way he told it. I wasn't there, and I mustn't judge, though others have expressed their incredulity, have wondered how he managed to escape jail. He caught the bottle in his left hand and hit it against her head, smashing the unbroken end that she had been holding. He dragged it downwards, cutting her forehead, cutting her eye, cutting her cheek. With his right hand he hit her. And then with his left. He hit her so hard he broke two of his fingers. Such ferocity. Where did it come from? He'd never play again. She'd never look the same.

Twenty-eight

More and more I found it hard to see him. I was thinking of telling him to find someone else, saying I thought we'd gone as far as we could. I remembered a time in the past when we'd meet and for a couple of days I'd feel completely elated. Then we'd meet again and something would have happened – he'd have got drunk and abusive, thrown out of some bar; or he'd storm in, get aggressive, storm out again – and after he left I'd find myself feeling shell-shocked, bombarded, like he'd given me concussion. I'd be down and grumpy and despairing, not knowing what to do for him; and then I'd forget it. I'd get on with my life. I'd be fine until we next met and the whole horrid process started again. Now, I didn't even get those first few days of elation. Now, all Lee did was make me miserable. I was an addict whose fix is a necessity rather than a high. I had to cut him out.

Twenty-nine

On Sunday evening James rang up. He left a message. He said, 'With things as they are it's probably best if you move out. I'll come round in the week and we can discuss it.'

'What is he playing at?' Lee asked me on Monday. 'Why is he doing this?

'I've got to get him,' Lee was saying, 'I've got to nail him. He's taken everything away from me. That bedsit job, that was my break . . . Gina . . . God, I could have had something with Gina. Life was about to be great. I just *know* he told her to come home that morning, knew she'd catch me with Lara. If only she hadn't come home . . .'

He found himself standing on shaky foundations. Not only the present but his past came under attack. The last fifteen years, he had to rewrite them. It wasn't his parents' desires had brought him to this point or this point, nor Cabresi's, nor Lizzie's, but James's. 'It's all James isn't it, Peter? You knew it was, didn't you? You kept trying to tell me.'

But I thought, Don't we all use a strategy to get what we want? Isn't it impossible to tell who is controlling and who being controlled? He who seems taken in by your generosity, your kindness, your flattery, isn't he merely another manipulator? Rewarding your actions as a means to direct your behaviour. They are both as bad as each other.

'Was it Gina, is that what he wanted? He got what he wanted. I can't stand the thought of it,' he said, 'them together. It's in my head, it wakes me up. Who's there?

Who's there for me? James was my best friend – Gina . . .
Even my parents – Cabresi – anyone I've ever loved—'

Thirty

Finally, it began to impinge, the sense that he was utterly
alone. He had watched things crash down around him but
while they were actually crashing he had been shielded by
his outrage, his exasperation, his guilt, his regret. When
very excited, positively or negatively, it is impossible to
experience depression, when adrenaline levels are high,
and stimulating. Once he'd come up with his plan he
was manic again, but for now, he was resigned, deflated,
dull . . .

'I can't go outside,' he says to me, 'I'm afraid of outside.
And I'm scared of *myself*, feeling like that, I've felt that
before. It's just that they live round the corner. I don't want
them to see me.' When he thinks about them, he tells me, his
spine tightens and his tongue sticks fast to his palate. *When*
he thinks about them? He thinks about them all the time,
Gina and James and his job and his home, and nothing is
safe. People give things with one hand and take them away
with the other. His shoulders calcify backwards. His chest
opens to the elements.

It scared him, this feeling, this tightness, it preceded
absence of feeling and he'd been there before. He didn't
think he wanted to come back from this, to put himself
together, to like the effect, to find his home and embark
upon another career, to feel himself fill up with optimism.
It was an illusion, well-being. There was only so long he

could make these things real. He didn't see the point. He didn't have the will.

'I've started over once,' he said. 'I don't think I can do it again.'

I agreed with him.

I said, 'You're right. I don't think you can either. You're your own worst enemy, Lee. Even *I've* thought lately we should end these sessions, I've thought, there's nothing further I can do . . .'

'I fucked up, I really fucked up,' he said. 'Jesus! Tell me it won't be like this forever.

'I wake up in the morning and I know what they think of me. It sticks to me. I feel sick all day. I feel disgusting. I go to bed. I get up the next morning. Tell me it won't be like this forever.

'Help me, Peter.

'It's been the same my whole life. That's why I can't look forward. It'll be the same again. I know it will. It'll happen again. Whatever I touch.'

I couldn't help feeling he was right. I could have helped *saying* it, but I was feeling spiteful. And anyway, listening to his disintegration, watching it, I was utterly detached. In the midst of some great crisis it is all-consuming but to anyone outside, it is utterly ridiculous. The great business of broken hearts and failing friendships, of misunderstandings and injuries, the things that keep people awake while everyone else is sleeping soundly, so personal, so insignificant, so silly. Perhaps that's why I said it. And perhaps that's why I helped him with his plan. It seemed part of this same stupid nonsense, this drama. It didn't seem real.

He didn't seem real, the way he shuffled to keep our appointments thereafter, the slight tremor that started in his hands, the lowness of his voice, its quietness, the monotone of his face. It was a bizarre form of déjà vu. He was entirely as he'd been when I'd first met him, but suddenly I didn't care. The thing he'd always accused me of had finally come true. (What we fear we find.) All his accusations, I noticed, had been true – I *had* thought my way better than his, I *had* tried to get him to be my creature. Well, he hadn't complied and look at him now. He could do what he wanted. As far as I was concerned, it was up to him.

But what he wanted was to die.

Thirty-one

The cessation of pain I understand, but with Lee it wasn't so simple. There was a clause attached, the bring-James-down clause, which implied a contest, a winning and a losing and necessarily, therefore, some kind of con-tinuing. Fundamentally, unconsciously, Lee believed him-self immortal. I could see it in the fire in his eyes once he'd come up with his plan. Life took on a sweetness. Perhaps as he was leaving it behind. Some premature nostalgia.

I thought I had contemplated suicide before but listening to his scheming I had such a vision of its reality that I felt something like pure pleasure for a moment. The surety that life would end was comforting, the certainty that every minute I was deciding to live, a relief. As soon as he'd decided, he regained his strength, there was purpose in his actions, who was I to take that away?

Thirty-two

He started describing scenarios with his usual vigour. James had been to see him—

'He came round with cans of lager, can you believe it, like it was some fucking social call, and then he told me I'd got two weeks to leave. But what the fucker didn't count on was beer cans with his fingerprints all over them, I even got a glass, the idiot, because he asked for some water, so now we've got him. We'll do the bar tonight. We've got a perfect excuse to do it tonight.'

'I'm seeing a friend tonight.'

'Who?'

'His name is Joseph.'

'That doesn't matter, bring him along.'

Thirty-three

Some other thing has overtaken me. Something like purpose. I'm going to do this thing. I'm going to do one thing by which the rest of my life will be defined. The one thing that, if people knew, they'd remember me for. How often does that happen?

Thirty-four

It is as easy as this.

'I used to come to this part of town a lot when I was

younger. I found it very exciting. But I don't come so often any more.'

'Why not?'

'I *am* still a member of the Orange Room.'

'Really?'

'I go there occasionally.'

'I've never been. I'd love to.'

'We'll go after this if you like. Have a quick drink.'

'Can we?'

'Sure.' He looked all nervous and excited. '—There's nothing special about it. It's just a place like any other.'

James is at the bar and the blood goes hot in my head. It is as easy as this. Any second now Lee will arrive.

He did. He'd worked himself up to an excellent anger. His face was dark, his shoulders trembled . . .

It was the first time I'd seen them together and it was an odd sensation. Did I make it up or did I sense their utter knowledge of each other? It wasn't a real situation. It was over very quickly.

Time seemed to speed up. He'd said his piece, he'd threatened James and then he'd left almost before I'd witnessed it. It all happened so quickly.

Thirty-five

Two days later I went round to his house. I remember it in technicolour. Lee, bright around the edges, letting me in through a bright green door. He didn't wait for any sort of greeting but turned in immediately, back to his lair. Hanging in the hall was a picture of him behind his cello which I wanted to look at but he'd marched on ahead of me into the kitchen. He offered me a cup of tea. There were photos pinned to some cork and I wondered if Bob and Nancy were among them, I didn't know what they looked like, I wondered if I ever would. Now, though, wasn't the time to mention it. He offered me the cup of tea again and I accepted. I was surprised to find that he only had herbal. I was surprised that he offered it to me, filled up the kettle, took out a mug from the cupboard, all so normally, as though this was any old day, this was any old visit; but what did I expect? From him, dramatics. Then, maybe, this was most dramatic of all.

I'd brought some surgical gloves with me and I wanted to put them on before I touched something inadvertently, but it seemed rude to get them out of my bag. It seemed sick to take them out, snap them on, grotesquely funny. I sat with my hands in my lap, I didn't drink the tea he gave me.

What on earth was I thinking? What on earth was I thinking as I followed him into the sitting room, sat beside him on the sofa, listened as he talked through the exactness of what we'd planned? He'd put James's glass by the side of an armchair, vaguely out of sight; the cans of lager he'd brought round, both empty and full, were on a low table in front of us. 'I've purposefully not drunk all day,' he said, 'I've purposefully not taken anything – I don't think I should before 7.30 when he's supposed to come round.' I took out my gloves. 'Jesus,' he said. 'It's all right,' I said, 'I haven't touched anything yet.'

Thirty-six

'I want to do this, Peter, I'm so excited about this,' he said, like an idiot. 'In this can I'm just going to put a couple of Rohypnol because I don't want to crash out immediately, I want to enjoy it.' He grinned. I wondered what it would be like tomorrow. Him gone. Out of my life, my head. Perhaps I loved him so much I'd do anything for him. Perhaps I thought it would mean something, that we'd be forever connected. I'd felt a collusion with him since he involved me in his plan that I'd never felt before. Tonight, too, there was a closeness, we were both on the same side. He reminded me to throw everything away afterwards.

He lay on the floor, relaxing, eyes closing, drifting to sleep, all that Rohypnol talking nonsense. I knelt down beside him, rolled up his sleeve, touched his arm, the first time I'd touched him, such soft skin. I waited. God knows how long I waited, watched him sleeping. Then I knelt on his arm, knees either side of his elbow joint, elbow pressed into the ground, the soft skin where his arm bends, stretched, those two veins underneath it juicy and fat, the needle went in with the force of my body; I paused, how long would it take? a minute? five? ten? A convulsion. Panic in Lee's body. A seizure. A fit. A horrible gasping for life. But small display for what's been extinguished. All *that*, those years, those loves, those ideas, this stillness . . .

Thirty-seven

After some time I stood up and wandered towards the hall. I leant against the doorframe; I realized I was breathing in. This was what his house smelled like. I walked towards the kitchen in slow motion, touching the walls, almost floating, as though I was the one who had died. He'd painted the kitchen himself, the cornering-off was uneven. I sat on one of the chairs at the square wooden table. I felt empty, light, a thing of nothingness. Straight ahead, when my eyes had focused, I was looking through French windows into the garden. Dark out there. I'd never seen the garden. For how long I don't know, I sat there and looked at the garden.

The chest of drawers to my left caught my attention. It lifted my spirits in some mysterious way, as if I'd find him within it, find some secret. I started riffling through. Inside were neatly stacked folders, each neatly titled in Lee's round writing: bank statements, bills, payslips, the financial year. For a second it struck me that I had a whole house to look through and it was an instant of something wonderful before it was just an instant that vanished again. I went through the house nonetheless.

I stayed with him until about two in the morning. Partly because I couldn't bear to leave him, partly because I was afraid someone would see me. I heard James arrive and ring the bell at half past nine. Lee was just over an hour dead by then.

Thirty-eight

In moments of self-doubt, dark moments, I imagine a room filled with people, mostly strangers to each other, people who've been dotted around my life. Just those who I've lied to, hurt, let down or betrayed. I imagine them discovering their common link, suppose their conversation turning to me, their various descriptions . . . What a hideous chimera. But there is one thing about me that none of them knows. However bad they might think me, manipulative, mean, they don't know the worst thing about me, they still have a higher opinion of me than I deserve. I find some comfort in that.

With thanks to

Giles Smart, Don Warrington, Paul Cooper,
Jeremy Cooper, Ella & Finn McCreath, Marcus Wayland,
Alex Sullivan, Bruce Hunter, Carol MacArthur, Jon Butler,
Josef Gardiner, Venetia Butterfield, M & D.

Vanessa Jones

Twelve

'Measured and elegant, *Twelve* is a thoroughly intriguing novel studded with thoughtful and witty insights, and I've never read a novel before that contained both ecstasy trips and gardening tips.' ARTHUR SMITH

'Lily's lifestyle is an enviable one, but she is unhappy – alienated, disaffected and bored. When a man hands her a note on the Tube bearing his name and number, she rings him in the hope of an adventure. *Twelve* takes us on several involving, interior journeys, frequently giving us passages of virtuoso writing. Comparisons can be invidious , but *Twelve* could be seen as a book narrated by a more intelligent, self-aware and literary Bridget Jones, with the journals of some of her close friends thrown in.' *Time Out*

'*Twelve* is distinguished by flashes of fine writing. Vanessa Jones clearly has a deep understanding of the generation she describes. She is a writer of genuine promise.'

Daily Telegraph

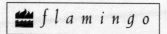 *flamingo*

Patrick Gale

Rough Music

Julian as a small boy is taken on the perfect Cornish holiday. With the arrival of glamorous American relations emotions run high and events spiral out of control. Though he has been brought up in the forbidding shadow of the prison his father runs, though his parents are neither as normal nor as happy as he supposes, Julian's world view is the sunnily selfish, accepting one of boyhood. It is only when he becomes a man – seemingly at ease with love, with his sexuality, with his ghosts – that the traumatic effects of that distant summer rise up to challenge his defiant assertion that he is happy and always has been.

'Gripping, elegant and wise, it is Gale's best book to date, and should not be missed.' *Independent*

'A fabulously unnerving book . . . a hugely compelling writer.' *Independent on Sunday*

'Like the sea he describes so well, Patrick Gale's clear, unforced prose sucks one in effortlessly.' *Daily Mail*

'A marvellous, page-turning, edge-of-your-seat story . . . there are no false notes in this book.' *Marie Claire*

'It would be churlish to divulge more of the plot; suffice to say that it is as ingenious in design as it is generous in spirit.' *Sunday Express*

ISBN: 0 00 655220 X

 *flamingo*

Maria McCann

As Meat Loves Salt

'A fat, juicy masterpiece . . . the pages flow like claret.'
Economist

'Early in the English Civil War, a body is dredged from the
pond of a Royalist estate. *As Meat Loves Salt* is the testament
of Jacob Cullen – homicide and fugitive . . . McCann is a
marvellous storyteller. A certain splendour in the writing
makes this novel a *tour de force* of sensational scenes, an
anatomy of violence and an elegy for lost kinship. Rich in
secrets and surprises, this novel has its own fierce poetry.'
Independent

'An outstanding novel, fresh and unusual [with] all the dirt,
stink, rasp and flavour of the time.' *Daily Telegraph*

'An intriguing and disturbing first novel which lingers in
the mind . . . Tense with anguish, intimacy and shame, it
imaginatively re-creates the mentality of a society racked by
war and intoxicated by radical new ideas of freedom and
change.' *TLS*

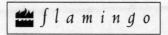

Grant Stewart

The Octopus Hunter

'Excellent, disturbing . . . A first-rate thriller that plugs into the insanities of our age.'
Tribune

'This exciting novel pulls no punches in its depiction of the brutality of war and shows the fragility of a land and its people when gun law takes over. A vivid tale.'   *What's On*

'Stewart brings the Balkan hotpot of ethnic struggle to the parameters of Western understanding through the eyes of a young traveller who buys a hotel on the Albanian coast, hoping to bring in a few adventurous tourists. Instead Robert finds himself on the fringes of a war zone. Charting a nation's ferocious war cry and a foreigner's voice from within it, *The Octopus Hunter* examines the dangerous lure of conflict.'
The Latest

'Stewart transplants Conrad's *Heart of Darkness* to south-eastern Europe and by the time the Serbs arrive Robert has changed from Marlowe to Kurtz, unable to tell right from wrong. The horror duly arrives on his doorstep.'   *GQ*

'This exciting novel pulls no punches in its depiction of the brutality of war and shows the fragility of a land and its people when gun law takes over. A vivid tale.'   *What's On*

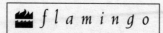

Magnus Mills

The Restraint of Beasts

Shortlisted for the Booker Prize and the Whitbread First Novel Award

Meet Tam and Richie: two dour Scots labourers. Fond of denim, workshy, permanently discontented, intent on getting to the pub every night come hell or high water – in short, just your average workmen. But Tam and Richie, with their new supervisor, begin to display hidden depths. Despatched to a farmsite in England by their boss Donald, they deal conclusively with first one then another client, all the while sticking unbendingly to their rituals until comeuppance arrives to herd them away. But just who exactly are the Hall Brothers, and what do they farm?

'A demented, deadpan comic wonder.' THOMAS PYNCHON

'Mills's first novel really is good . . . The terseness of his vocabulary produces an effect that is oblique and elliptical, yawning with sinister implication, in a manner which may be called Kafkaesque . . . a forceful and original first novel, clever and funny and rewardingly strange.'
JENNY TURNER, *Independent on Sunday*

ISBN: 0 00 655114 9

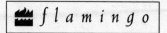 *flamingo*

Agnès Desarthe

Five Photos of My Wife

'A subtle and sly dissection of love, loss and truth . . . Full of charm and imagination, and darkly funny, too.' *Elle*

Still reeling from the death of his beloved wife Telma, old Max Opass writes to his daughter with news of his empty days and humdrum activities – and tells her that he's decided to have Telma's likeness committed to canvas. To start with, he looks up 'Artists' in the Yellow Pages, picks a few at random, and commissions each to produce a portrait of his wife, working from five snapshot photographs for reference. But while one artist intimidates Max, another prompts him to pity; a pair of art students baffle him; and a bridge-playing acquaintance turns out to have the elderly hots for him. And with each subsequent moving, sometimes comic encounter, the reader comes to realize that Max's grasp on who his wife really was perhaps is not so sure after all . . .

'A rare tribute to the love of a wife . . . Desarthe's gentle novel, lucidly translated by Adriana Hunter, is the kind of mood piece at which the French excel. While many kinds of art are evoked (acrylic, oils, collage and video), her own prose suggests a watercolour – delicate, subtle and full of charm.'
MICHAEL ARDITTI, *Daily Mail*

'Well told, elegantly conceived and constructed'
DOMINIC BRADBURY, *The Times*

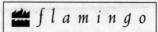 *flamingo*